ISLAND OF THE WHITE ROSE

ISLAND OF THE WHITE ROSE

ISLAND OF THE WHITE ROSE

A Novel

R. Ira Harris

Bridge Works Publishing Company
Bridgehampton, New York

Published by Bridge Works Publishing Company, Bridgehampton, New York. Distributed in the United States by National Book Network, Lanham, Maryland. For descriptions of this and other Bridge Works books, visit the website at www.BridgeWorksBooks.com.

FIRST EDITION

Library of Congress Cataloging-in-Publication Data

Harris, R. Ira, 1947–
    Island of the white rose : a novel / R. Ira Harris.—First edition.
        pages cm
        ISBN 978-0-9816175-5-8 (cloth print edition : alk. paper)
        ISBN 978-0-9816175-6-5 (e-book)
        1. Cuba—History—Revolution, 1959—Underground movements—Fiction. 2. Historical fiction. 3. Love stories. I. Title.
PS3608.A783267I85 2013
813'.6—dc23
                        2012049600
                10 9 8 7 6 5 4 3 2 1

To my parents who taught me to love books,
and to Suncita who inspired me to write this one.

ISLAND OF THE WHITE ROSE

ISLAND OF THE WHITE ROSE

Chapter 1

Eighteen Lightning-class sloops cut through the waves of the Florida Straits like a school of porpoises, first all in one direction and then, in a flash of billowing sail, another, as each rounded a course buoy. It was the first race of the summer season, and each boat was skippered by a member of the Havana Yacht Club. The sailors, the upper crust of Havana society, were the businessmen and professionals who thrived in the booming Cuban economy.

The boats neared the finish in a close reach. Not more than a few boat lengths separated the first three. The skipper of the second-place Lightning was Father Pedro Villanueva. The youngest son of a wealthy family, Pedro was thirty-three years old and dressed in madras swim shorts and a polo shirt emblazoned "HYC." Nothing about his appearance suggested his occupation. His racer hiked steeply, and he leaned his six-foot frame out as far as he could to counterbalance the wind. His boat flew across the choppy water.

Shoving the tiller to port, he started his homeward tack. He could see that the windows of the yacht club reflected the setting sun, a brilliant pink-and-orange glow. Pedro loved this time of day when nature electrified the world with its splendor. Closing in on the lead, he yanked on the main sheet and adjusted the trim. The gap narrowed, but the finish line was fast approaching. He'd have to settle for second. Still, the sunset was a perfect consolation.

As the race ended, Pedro spotted a young woman clad in a red bikini, laughing and drinking on the deck of the commodore's launch. As he crossed its bow, she smiled down at him, then tossed her head and turned back to her friends. Her swimsuit caught Pedro's eye. Not many women at the club were brazen enough to sport such attire. Perhaps the bikini-clad beauty was a movie-star friend of a member. He was certain she'd be the talk of the dining room that night.

Pedro's family had been members of the club since the 1930s, and he knew everyone there. It was the chicest of the elite clubs that dominated Havana's social life. Its members prided themselves on the fact that even President Fulgencio Batista did not qualify for membership. The club was for whites only. Batista, part Indian, white, and Chinese, lacked the necessary pedigree. Still, Cuba was a beautiful place to live if you were white and had money. For those who could afford it, the island was an international playland, with Hollywood stars in attendance at casino shows that rivaled the best of Las Vegas.

Having grown up around boats, Pedro could race and often beat the best sailors in the club. In a race, if the wind shifted, he instinctively adjusted the trim. In the doldrums, he had the skill to watch for the ripples that signaled the arrival of a fresh breeze and to anticipate the wind's first breaths. When he wasn't racing, the sea was the perfect place to reflect on his life on land—a life that he found increasingly disconsolate.

On the nights Pedro spent at the club, he rubbed elbows with dozens of beautiful women who sparkled in the candlelight. After five years in the priesthood, the vow of celibacy weighed heavily upon him. He watched longingly as these unattainable jewels adorned the arms of their escorts or danced to the music on the terrace overlooking the sea. His vows stopped him from engaging in anything beyond polite chitchat but, in his heart, he wanted to flirt, to tease, to be just like everyone else.

That Pedro Villanueva had entered the priesthood had come as no surprise to anyone. From the time Tomás—Pedro's oldest brother—had been a child, his father, Dr. Hugo Villanueva, had pushed him to join his busy obstetrical practice. Alberto, the second born, was destined to be a lawyer, the profession of his maternal grandfather. That left the church for Pedro, child number three. The boys' mother, Asunción Villanueva, went to the Iglesia de Jesús de Miramar for Mass and prayed for her children, but most of all, she prayed that Pedro would be her gift to God.

After showering, Pedro ambled over to the terrace to find his parents. His normally pale skin was sunburned from the race, and his black Brylcreemed hair was parted sharply to the side. He had changed from shorts to his black tunic and white collar. Apart from the collar, he was a study in black, relieved only by a glittering gold cross hanging from a chain around his neck.

A band was playing to a dance floor full of revelers lost in the rhythm of a mambo. Dinner was formal, with women in cocktail dresses and men in either guayabera shirts and white slacks or black tuxedos. They barely noticed the enormous roar of the cannon fired from La Cabaña, the ancient fortress looming over Havana Bay that now served as a prison. The detonation signaled nine P.M., just as it had done each night since the eighteenth century. Pedro winced, but no one else reacted to the explosion, and the party didn't skip a beat. His parents, as usual, looked as stiff as the mannequins from El Encanto department store, the Saks Fifth Avenue of Havana. His brother Alberto was wearing a tux, and Alberto's wife, Alejandra, was wearing a strapless dress that captured Pedro's attention. My lucky brother, he thought.

The mambo ended, and the band took up a *danzón*, the sensuous national dance of Cuba. Pedro focused on a woman gliding across the floor in her partner's arms. She was wearing a strapless red dress with a high slit on the side. She shook her shoulders in a provocative shimmy, her breasts a hair's breadth from her partner's chest, her hips swinging out a little farther than the other women, and her glance slightly chillier. Soon, the other dancers moved to the side, seemingly mesmerized by the sensual moves of this crimson vixen.

Pedro was captivated, too. He quickly realized that she was the woman in the bikini. Women can be so beautiful, he thought wistfully. He whispered in Alberto's ear, asking if he knew who this creature was. Alberto did not disappoint, providing a hurried précis on the vision in red. She was Dolores Barré, the daughter of Ricardo Barré, a United Fruit Company lawyer whom Alberto had assisted in times past. Dolores had attended graduate school at Cal Poly in San Luis Obispo, California, after earning a degree in electrical engineering at the Universidad Central "Marta Abreu" de Las Villas. Intelligent *and* sexy, thought Pedro. He sighed deeply.

Now, Pedro stared baldly at Dolores, taken by her energy and the bounce of her wavy, dark-brown hair. With so many Don Josés vying for her attention on the dance floor, she reminded Pedro of a modern-day Carmen. All she lacked was a rose in her teeth. Dolores's effortless ease as the center of attention reminded Pedro of Isabel, his first and only love.

Damn it, he thought to himself. After all these years he'd finally stopped looking for her at the club where they'd danced, the beach where the waves hid their embraces, and the cafés near the university where they'd talked for hours—but it didn't take much to bring it all back. Isabel's big ideas to replace Batista with a soviet-style government, to denounce her record-producer father and the wealth that he stood for, had finally ended their relationship. There was no room in her world for him, so religion became his fallback.

Pedro continued to watch Dolores gyrate on the floor and followed her with his eyes when she walked off. As she sauntered by their table, Pedro stood up and Alberto introduced his brother.

"Your dancing was exquisite," Pedro said as she extended her hand. Dolores smiled at the praise, and draped her left hand on his shoulder. As they talked, she played delicately with his collar, as if she were a moth and he the light. Pedro moved a step back.

"Now, Father, don't be so shy," she teased. "You're still a man under that collar." Pedro's face reddened.

"I've embarrassed you; I'm so sorry."

Perspiration formed on Pedro's forehead and above his upper lip. He quickly introduced Dolores to his parents and his sister-in-law, who were looking at them in astonishment.

"Your son's quite the skipper. At the end he was gaining like a son of a bitch. I thought he'd take the lead, but the damn finish line came up too quickly."

Dolores broke into a dazzling smile. Pedro thought she had the face of a porcelain doll—flawless skin with high cheekbones and perfectly shaped lips.

Asunción blanched at Dolores's language, but her gaiety was infectious. "Oh, listen to my mouth! There I go again. I'm embarrassing all of you." Another couple jostled its way onto the dance floor behind Dolores, pushing her forward and pressing her up against Pedro's chest.

"No, my dear," said Pedro's father with an amused grin. "We're all here to enjoy ourselves, too."

Turning to Pedro, he said, "Padre, you better think up a long list of penances if you're going to save Dolores's soul!" The table erupted in laughter, with the exception of Asunción.

Antonio Gonzáles, a club director and the skipper who'd won the regatta that afternoon, approached the table and asked Dolores to dance. Pedro quickly sat down and grabbed his drink. As the trumpets growled and the bongos beat out a distinctive rhythm, the two dancers disappeared into a crowd doing the cha-cha.

Three bone-chilling blasts of a whistle pierced the hubbub. An army officer dressed in yellow khakis led a squad of steel-helmeted soldiers onto the terrace. Their carbines at the ready, the soldiers plunged the party into a dark and threatening silence. The music ground to a stop, and the dancers turned to statues.

"Everybody stay where you are!" ordered the officer. Pedro sat motionless until Asunción dropped a glass of champagne she was about to sip, sending shards of glass flying around her feet. The racket on the terrace silenced to a low murmur. The officer scanned the diners and servers, then scrutinized the dancers. He moved his gaze back to a busboy holding a serving tray in shaking hands. The young man bent down and fumbled with the tray, leaning it against the wall, then stood up and remained stock-still, eyes averting the searchers. The officer blew his whistle and pointed at the busboy, who frantically ran toward the maître d'.

"Please tell them I'm innocent!" the busboy screamed.

The soldiers surrounded the hapless man, one wrestling him to the floor. Others attacked him with batons until two of the soldiers picked him up and dragged him down to the beach and out of sight. The officer and the rest of the squad turned without a word, roughly pushing club members aside.

For a moment, there was a sepulchral silence on the terrace, until the bandleader quickly struck up the music and the dancing resumed. The crowd began to sing, undisturbed by the violence they'd just witnessed: *"¡Mambo, que rico el Mambo. Mambo, que rico es, es, es!"*

The party began anew. Pedro noted Dolores and her escort, still showing off on the dance floor, and his family smiling and joking with friends at neighboring tables. He saw that life was back to normal, and the speed with which it had returned was unnerving. Nothing was going to stop the party, at least not tonight.

The band changed to a slow tune, *Cómo Fue*, one of Pedro's favorites. *"How did it happen? I can't tell you how it happened. I can't explain it. But I fell in love with you."*

This evening's party, like many others Pedro had attended at the Havana Yacht Club, would last until the wee hours of the morning. He got up and said goodnight to his family and departed alone, as always. The last thing he saw was the red dress swaying to the music. What had become of the world that a violent beating could be so quickly forgotten and seemingly normal people could go back to their revelry.

Pedro walked out into the warm night. It was just a ten-minute drive home through the streets of Old Havana to his apartment next to Iglesia del Espíritu Santo. There would be no dancing there.

Chapter 2

Pedro awoke early the next morning to incessant pounding on the door of his apartment. The clock on his night table showed that it wasn't quite seven. Groggy, he stumbled to the door and unlatched it. Father Domingo Goicoechea burst into the room. He'd been Pedro's childhood priest, and later, his advisor at the seminary. Pedro had grown accustomed to Domingo's showing up unbidden at his door, although usually it was at an hour of the day when Pedro's eyes were fully open.

Domingo, as always, needed a shave. He was short and round, and in the tropical heat, perpetually wiped the sweat from his brow. Once at the seminary, Pedro had seen him fall asleep during Mass; it was only when the music director walked over and "accidentally" stepped on his foot that Domingo had regained consciousness.

"You look like shit, my young friend," noted Domingo, his eyes twinkling.

"I'm glad to see you, too." Pedro turned and stumbled into his miniscule kitchen to fumble with the *moka* pot. "I had a late night, and I still have cobwebs in my eyes."

"Do you realize that it's seven o'clock? There's work to be done!"

"Work? Father, it's Saturday. What work?"

"You think you should only do your job on Sunday?" Domingo asked. "Most office workers are home today with their families."

"That's right, Domingo," said Pedro. "They are home—in bed!"

"Go call on them. See their kids play baseball. No wonder no one comes to your services."

Pedro's cheeks flushed as Domingo's words sank in. "Who says no one comes to my services?" he demanded.

"My son, we live in a fishbowl. You sneeze in Espíritu Santo and the archbishop interrupts his Mass five miles away to say 'God Bless you.'"

"Did the archbishop send you here to torment me this morning?" asked Pedro. "If he did, you're doing a wonderful job." Pedro managed to get the coffeepot operational, and the aroma of strong Cuban coffee started to waft through his apartment.

"No, no, no. I'm here to torment you out of the goodness of my heart," said Domingo. "Do you have any tostadas to go with that? You can't drink coffee without something to dunk; it's a sacrilege."

"I thought you were on a diet," Pedro said, glancing at Domingo's ample waistline.

"What are you, my doctor? I come here to help you develop your parish, and what do I get? Criticism!"

Domingo rummaged around the kitchen looking for something to eat. Spying some leftover cake, he sniffed it like a cautious dog and wolfed it down.

"You haven't heard a word I've said, have you?" Pedro asked.

"Of course, I have. You worry about me like an old woman."

"That's the prerogative of a former student. Where is it written that *I* should not worry about *you*?"

"Well, I don't worry about *you*, my skinny friend. I did not come here on Saturday just because I happened to be in the neighborhood. Your sainted mother approached me last week. She frets that you do not appear happy with your assignment. She wonders if you would prefer being in some other job and asked if I could use my influence to get you a more desirable posting."

Pedro walked over to the kitchen window, coffee cup in hand, and looked down to the street lined with pastel Spanish-colonial buildings. The majority of his parish lived above those stores. Five years serving this church, he thought, living next to it, is it worth it? He turned his head to the left and stared at the campanile's granite stone, filthy with a shroud of soot. The bell tower stood straight and true, an enduring symbol of the four hundred-year-old Catholic Church in Cuba. But what exactly did it stand for? he wondered. In Batista's Cuba, the archdiocese had made it clear that the clergy should tend to their flock and steer clear of politics. Pedro's church was a shining example of apathy to both the repressive regime in the presidential palace and the revolution that rumbled in the distance.

Cuba's central plateau and the Sierra Maestra were the main battlegrounds for Fidel Castro's revolution, but it occasionally erupted onto the streets of Havana and other major cities of the island. The war had been going on since 1956, and Castro's rebel forces, which numbered in the hundreds, battled Batista's poorly led but well-equipped army of twenty thousand. From time to time, terrorist bombs went off in the cities, but rarely any street-to-street fighting in Havana. Nothing at all hinted at revolution in the streets surrounding Pedro's church. Following the archdiocese's directive, he'd said nothing about either one from its pulpit.

Waking from his reverie, Pedro saw that Domingo was waiting for a response. "Dear God, protect me from my mother!" Pedro exclaimed. He flashed back to her constant entreaties to become a priest. She hasn't stopped, he thought. My God, she's taken to managing my career. From childhood, the priesthood is what she wanted for me, and now as an adult, I'm being controlled through Domingo. No wonder her favorite TV show is *Father Knows Best*. She's just like Margaret Anderson dictating every action of her children. The show should have been called *Mother Knows Best*.

Pedro remembered how he had succumbed to his mother's pressure, believing that the priesthood could be his way of emulating his beloved father. As a priest, he could take care of people's spiritual needs, just as Dr. Hugo looked after their physical health. But Pedro struggled with constant loneliness. After Isabel, he realized that the affair had tantalized him with a brief glimpse of the comfort that intimacy and love could offer. Isabel abandoned him, and the church had not filled the emptiness he felt every single day.

"Domingo, I'm just not sure I'm cut out to be a priest. I don't seem to be making a difference to anyone who does manage to find his way past the door down there, but it's more than that. Last night I was at the yacht club after the regatta. The way I felt when I looked at the women—that's not the way a priest is supposed to feel. There was one in a red dress that I couldn't take my eyes off. I wanted to hold her, to dance with her like anyone else. The music was intoxicating."

"Are you sure it wasn't just the music that was intoxicating?" asked Domingo with a patient smile on his face. "I know the bartender over there, and he's got a heavy hand."

Pedro had just parted his lips to reply, when Domingo held up his hand to stop him. "I know this has never been an easy part of the priesthood for you."

As he had done a hundred times at the seminary, Domingo began to chide Pedro about their faith. "My friend, the priesthood is a calling. Priests should not marry because the Church needs its spiritual leaders to love *everyone*, not just one woman. Listen to your inner self, and you will make the right decision. Remember, the devil wears red, too."

Pedro had listened back at the seminary and had made the commitment, but now five years had passed, and he questioned if he'd heard correctly. Wasn't there always going to be a red dress to torment him?

Chapter 3

More than a month had passed since Pedro had fallen under Dolores's spell. His life was a routine defined by daily Masses, funerals, baptisms, and maintenance of the four hundred-year-old church. He hadn't much time for fantasizing.

Finally, he had some spare time, so early one Saturday morning, Pedro set out from the yacht club in a Lightning. There was no race and no bikini-clad Dolores watching him from the commodore's launch — just the joy of the cool ocean spray dousing him under the oppressive July sun. Sailing was a welcome reminder that the world was a bigger place than the confines of his church. On the sea he was free to be himself, with no one having any expectations, no pews to fill, and no mentors or families to disappoint. Perhaps all priests should learn to sail, he thought.

Still, the memories of Dolores's voluptuousness intruded into his consciousness. Even as he chastised himself, he hoped that their paths might cross again. He beat an early retreat from the club and returned to his apartment to prepare a sermon for the next day.

A small fan on his desk circulated but failed to cool the humid air. Pedro, still in his swimsuit, scribbled his thoughts for a homily. He stared at the framed photo of his family sitting on the desk. His mother, seated next to his father, looked proudly up at Pedro, dressed in his vestments, a newly minted priest.

He squirmed in his seat as he wrote about Galatians 5:16–21 and fidelity in marriage. Would *anyone* believe *anything* he said about resisting the temptations of the flesh? The image of Dolores's suggestive dancing flashed in Pedro's mind. He stared down at his notepad, then tore off the sheet, crumpled it into a baseball, and threw it at the trash can. It bounced against the rim and fell onto the floor.

He need not have worried. The church was half empty the next morning Unless there was a wedding attracting crowds to the church, his Sunday Masses rarely saw more than thirty-five worshippers in attendance. With so few there that day, and only eight souls taking the Eucharist, the services went quickly, and Pedro retired to his stuffy office earlier than usual. He loosened his collar and held a glass of ice water against his aching forehead. He reflected on the day's services and realized that Domingo was right about the empty pews. Why had he not realized how few parishioners came to him for guidance or to hear his thoughts on the relevancy of the Church's view on the perpetual virginity of Mary? Even if the archdiocese would allow him to speak out about politics, he admitted that he knew as little about the goals of Fidel Castro—his old

17

high school and college classmate—as he did about what was important in men's lives.

His thoughts were interrupted by the sudden reappearance of Domingo. It must be lunchtime, Pedro thought.

"As always, your timing is impeccable," he told his friend. "I was just about to make some coffee. Won't you join me? One of the sisters just left some fresh-baked cookies."

"Do I look like I ever turn down a treat?"

Pedro produced a pot of dark Cuban coffee. Domingo nearly disappeared into the soft cushioning of the overstuffed sofa Asunción had bought for her son. Pedro took a seat in a wood rocking chair, ready for a new lecture.

"So how's my favorite student?" Domingo asked.

"Frustrated. People just don't seem interested in coming to Mass. The church was half empty today." Pedro leaned forward, gesturing with his hands as he spoke. "You were right, but I don't think it's my fault. I think people are afraid to come out on the streets these days, if they don't have to. There's no telling when a bomb is going to go off from one of those M-26-7 terrorists."

Father Domingo struggled to reach for a large sugar cookie. He thrust his torso forward. Steadying himself, he captured his prey and collapsed backward into the pillows.

"My son, you are mistaken on two counts," he said

as he munched, then coughed. Cookie crumbs deposited themselves down the front of his cassock.

"First, the bombs are not M-26-7. Castro's July 26 movement is stuck in the mountains, penned up by the army. More likely the bombs are from the students, followers of that idiotic Communist, Echevarria, the one who tried to assassinate Batista. The revolution has nothing to do with your problem. We've been here four hundred years, and the church has always stayed out of politics."

Domingo took another bite and choked again. He sputtered, showering bits of cookie in Pedro's direction.

"Second, if people don't come to church, it's the priest's fault, not the congregants'."

"My fault?" asked Pedro. "I lead the same service you taught me, every week. How is it that it's my fault that people don't show up?" He thought longingly about the Lightning plunging through the coolness of Havana Bay.

"You just said the magic word: *show.* I think you must have been sleeping during some of your classes at the seminary," said Domingo sternly. "When you're up there on the altar, you're the star of the show—the main act in the drama that it's your job to produce each and every week. And as the producer, you have to market the performance—go out into the streets. Like I told you, visit everyone in the neighborhood. Hang out at the bodega. Be visible. Know who your congregants are. They're not going to come to church to see a stranger. You have to develop a following, an audience."

"So you're telling me I have to be a salesman—a barker at a carnival—a walking, talking advertisement?" Pedro said disdainfully.

Domingo gave his student a beatific smile. "No, my cynical friend, not a barker. A *friend*. You have to be *their* friend, someone who cares about them, so they'll care what you have to say at church each week."

"And that's it? I just have to be a friend, and the church will fill to overflowing?"

Domingo had polished off four cookies. "Is there more coffee? These are delicious, but a little dry—no, that's not all there is. In addition to being the producer, you're also the director of a stage play. The church is your basic scenery, but there are other dramatic elements—music for one. People love a good song. A music director can really make a huge difference in attendance. He recruits a choir from the congregation. With music, you'll have them tapping their feet in the pews."

"You make it sound so simple. But we don't have the budget for a music director."

"Ah, but you see, you can't afford *not* to have one. It will make all the difference."

"I guess the problem really is that I'm not convinced it's so important to fill up the church every week. Between the bombings here in Havana and the news reports of clashes between the army and the rebels, what's the point of it all?"

Domingo paused, as if trying to remember the rest

of his lecture. "Ah, the third thing you have to do is to be the star of the show. And if the star doesn't believe in himself, you could have Carmen Miranda on the altar singing 'Brasil' from the top of her lungs and still no one would show up."

Pedro had a vision of Carmen Miranda, adorned with bowls of fruit made into hats, cavorting in front of the congregation. He needed to get Domingo on the road. "Okay, I do feel defeated. But in spite of your rationale about me, I feel it's these bombs killing *Habaneros* in the theaters and cafés that make me depressed. Even at the yacht club, Batista's soldiers came marching in and nearly beat a busboy to death! Nothing in my training taught me how to explain how God permits such violence. How do I explain the horror, when I don't understand it myself? Tell me! If I had an explanation to offer, they might come and listen to me." He put his head in his hands, feeling sick at the obtuseness of his fat friend.

The sound of gentle tapping on his office door brought Pedro back to reality. It was just past noon, and no one, for any reason, approached the church until after siesta time. After a louder knock, Pedro opened the door to discover two parishioners, Flora and Tácito Olivos. Pedro ushered them into his office and introduced Father Domingo, who immediately announced he had to leave, but not before taking two more cookies. "For the road."

The Olivoses were two of the few regular attendees at Sunday Mass. Pedro had performed the marriage ceremony for their daughter, Lola. Tácito was a dock-worker; the sun had taken a terrible toll on his face, lining it with deep crags. The couple lived in a railroad flat on Empedrado, about a fifteen-minute walk down the narrow streets of Old Havana. Pedro didn't recall seeing them at morning Mass.

Flora had deep rings under her eyes, and Pedro could see she was in great distress.

"Oh, Father, it's terrible! Homero, my daughter Lola's husband, is in La Cabaña. You remember him?"

Pedro searched his memory. "Of course, I married them. But what happened? Why is he there?"

"He works for *La Prensa* as a typesetter. *La Prensa* ran a column saying that the elections were rigged, so the government sent in the police to arrest everyone in the newspaper office. He is such a gentle soul, and now they've imprisoned him." Flora convulsed into tears.

"And he didn't write the story?" Pedro asked.

"He just barely made it through ninth grade," said Tácito. "Homero's a good boy, but a writer? Not a chance in hell. Excuse me, Father—"

"Don't worry, Tácito," Pedro interrupted.

Tácito continued, "He just matches up the print blocks with the words of the typeset story and gets the blocks ready for the press."

"When was he arrested?" asked Pedro.

"Last night," Tácito replied. "They arrested every-one, including the janitor!"

"And he's already in La Cabaña?" asked Pedro. "I

22

thought prisoners were taken to the police station before arraignment."

"Oh Father," said Tácito. "Arraignment? Trial? There are no trials anymore. No arraignments. It's only to La Cabaña, and then to the wall!"

Flora's sobbing became a continuous moan, as if she were in physical pain. Tácito tried vainly to comfort her.

"Let's not assume the worst straight off," Pedro said with concern.

"If you don't have a patron, you're going to be fish food once you get into La Cabaña," said Tácito.

"I'll call my brother," said Pedro. "He's a lawyer. He'll know what to do."

Pedro reached for the phone and called Alberto. "He's where?" Pedro asked the voice on the other end of the conversation. Flora stopped breathing, momentarily. "He's playing tennis in this heat?" The sobs continued. "Tell that donkey of a husband of yours that I called and that he should meet me at the club after he's through pretending to be Jack Kramer."

Pedro put down the phone. "I'll meet my brother this evening and tell him about Homero. When I'm done, I'll come to your house."

"Tonight?" Flora asked.

"Yes, but I'm not sure what time. If I come by and the lights are out, I'll return tomorrow morning."

"Father, no one's going to be sleeping at our house tonight."

Pedro and his brother found a secluded table near the bar in the yacht club's flashy dining room. The room had few diners, as most were out on the terrace to be close to the band. It was blasting out show tunes, but the music was muffled inside and the brothers could talk without shouting. Pedro picked at the food on his plate.

"You going to eat that?" Alberto asked, pointing at the steak in front of Pedro. Without waiting for an answer, he stabbed the meat with his fork and transferred it to his plate.

"My advice is to stay out of this," Alberto warned. He raised his voice, but not so loud that a neighboring table could hear. "Nothing good can come of it."

"But the kid was setting type. He had no part in deciding what to write or what to print! Doesn't there have to be a trial? Doesn't he have to do something illegal?"

"These are extraordinary times, and President Batista has suspended habeas corpus. No way to get someone freed from detention through legal means." Alberto popped a morsel of steak into his mouth and groaned with pleasure. "You sure you don't want to eat this? It's delicious."

Pedro suddenly found his brother as annoying as Domingo. "It's hard enough *watching you* eat. I don't want to think what would happen if *I* actually ate it. It's so rare you could probably get it to walk around your plate!"

"Blood rare is the only way to eat steak!" Alberto insisted. He sat back, loosened his tie, and belched.

"Enough about food! I don't want to think about it."

Pedro looked out beyond the windows of the dining room at the ocean's indigo expanse, not able to see the waves rolling in, but taking comfort knowing that the sea was there, undisturbed by events on land. He looked back at his brother. "Do you mean there are *nonlegal* means to get someone out of prison? What are you not telling me?" Pedro demanded, his voice rising above the chatter of the dining room.

Guests at neighboring tables, attracted by Pedro's vehemence, turned toward them. Alberto raised his hand just above the edge of the table, making a warning gesture. "Pedro, you really don't want to ask such questions here. Remember, the—"

"If there's a way to save this boy, I want to do it," Pedro interrupted, tapping the table with his fingers.

"You have to be careful," Alberto cautioned in a voice now just above a whisper. "Around here, the walls have ears. Everything and everybody has a price nowadays. Finding out how much is the trick."

"Can you find out?"

"This is really important to you?"

"I wouldn't ask if it weren't. His in-laws are my parishioners."

"All right, all right, I'll make a few calls. I may have to talk to one or two people I know with links inside La Cabaña."

"You know people *inside* La Cabaña?"

"You don't want to know the people I know."

"Then for the love of God, talk to them."

"I'll see what I can find out," said Alberto. "And brother, at least drink some coffee so I won't feel like I'm eating alone."

There was no late-night stop at the Olivos house. Pedro knew they'd be up hoping for news, but he had none, and he shied away from confronting their disappointment. He would wait until he had something more definitive. In any case, he didn't have the energy to deal with Flora's misery.

Chapter 4

The following day, Pedro trudged through the burning July heat to the decaying second-story apartment where the Olivoses lived. The money that had been pouring into town for the hotel district hadn't filtered down to this distant quarter of Old Havana. Pedro, dressed in his long cassock, was careful where he stepped, as the streets were riddled with potholes, and rain had filled them with filthy runoff.

As he made his way along the streets, Pedro sought shade wherever he could, any relief from the sun. But there was nothing he could do to avoid the humidity that wrapped Havana like a Turkish bath. Mopping his forehead, he stepped into a pile of dung, a souvenir from one of the many mules that plied the streets transporting produce to market.

"*Mierda!*"

The smell turned his stomach. Scraping his soles on the stone curb failed to clean the shit off his shoes, and he arrived at the Olivoses wishing he'd never left the church. Flora dissolved into tears when he told her he had no news.

"But you said you would help!" she cried.

"I'm trying," Pedro assured her, wondering again why he'd gotten involved. Alberto had been right. Nothing good was going to come of this, he thought. Maybe the archbishop is right, too—the place for a priest is inside the walls of his church.

Pedro bade Flora a hurried farewell and walked quickly to where a taxi was parked. He jumped in, only too eager to escape the pestilential, baking streets.

Three days passed without a word, but finally Alberto called. He wanted to get out of his stuffy office. "Meet me at El Floridita, and for God's sake, don't wear a cassock or a collar!"

Pedro had been to El Floridita a few times before entering the seminary. Places like the touristy bar had been part of what Isabel had rejected when she'd broken off their romance. The watering hole, one of the oldest in all Havana, had become world-famous when Hemingway made its long mahogany bar his hangout. When Pedro arrived, waiters in red jackets were attending to the many American tourists who stood shoulder to shoulder at the bar. In dark slacks and an ivory guayabera shirt, Pedro resembled just another tourist looking for a party. He jostled his way through the crowded room until he found his brother seated in a corner booth. He was drinking a daiquiri, El Floridita's claim to fame.

Alberto wasted no time filling Pedro in. He'd been to a seedy café near the Malecón, Havana's oceanfront street, and had met with an off-duty guard from La Cabaña. "I think I was the only one in that pisshole who'd bathed in a week," said Alberto. "The place smelled like a century of spilled beer."

"What was the guard like?" asked Pedro.

"The human equivalent of a sewer rat. Not the kind of guy you'd bring to the club. He smelled as bad as he looked."

"Can he help?"

"I told you everything has a price. Yeah, he can help, but it's gonna cost five thousand U.S. dollars."

"What? How are we supposed to do that?" Pedro felt his stomach knot. What kind of mess have I started, making promises I can't keep? I should never have told Flora that there's hope.

A waiter came over to take his order. Pedro stared straight ahead, lost in his misery. Alberto pointed to his drink. "Bring my brother one of these, and I'll have another."

Alberto reached across the table and placed his hand on Pedro's wrist. "Listen, if this is what you want, I can make it happen."

Pedro heard the words, but they didn't register. "Five thousand dollars. Where am I going to get that kind of money? How am I going to face that family? What can I tell them?"

He stared at the Americans at the bar. They looked as if they'd have no trouble coming up with five thousand dollars. "What am I supposed to do, steal it from those gringos?" he asked, pointing to the crowd hoisting their drinks, toasting each other in life's big party.

Alberto took a long sip of his daiquiri. His straw made a loud sucking sound as the drink vanished from the glass. He repeated his offer.

"Are you nuts?" Pedro gasped. "You can spare five grand?"

"Listen, my friend, I never took a vow of poverty. All these casinos moving into town, all these Americans with all their dollars, the bosses at United Fruit with all their contracts—a lawyer would have to be deaf, dumb, and blind for some of those dollars not to find their way into his pocket. This economy is booming, and so is my bank account! And don't forget Tomás. When he became a doctor, they didn't make *him* take a vow of poverty, either. Personally, I think you're crazy to get involved with this situation, but if that's what you want, I'm here to help you."

Pedro took a moment to consider Alberto's proposal. He'd never thought about his brothers' professions, and what they did for a living. Alberto was four years older than Pedro. When they were kids, Pedro thought Alberto knew how to do everything. He was faster on a bike and on roller skates. A better swimmer. Alberto had preceded him at the Belén school, and every time Pedro had a problem with a subject, the Jesuits reminded him how smart his older brother was. Worse than that—they reminded him how smart *both* his brothers were.

Tomás was two years older than Alberto and had been an undisputed genius at school, but it was Alberto whose abilities encompassed both academics and sports. When I was a boy, Pedro thought to himself, there was nothing he couldn't do, and now—there's still nothing he can't do. Pedro grabbed Alberto's hand. "You have money for this?" Pedro uttered a rapid prayer. "I had no idea—"

"It's only money, Padre," Alberto said with a smile. "A helluva lot of money, but not the end of the world."

"What's the next step?" Pedro asked.

Alberto told him that a meeting had been set up for the following week and that it would take both of them to handle the transaction. Pedro reached for the daiquiri sitting in front of him. "I think I need something stronger than this," he murmured, bypassing the straw and taking a big gulp.

Pedro thought back. It had been less than a week since the Olivoses had first deposited their grief on his doorstep, and in only a few days more he was going to retrieve Homero from the dark maw of La Cabaña.

Trying to save Homero was the first time Pedro had looked beyond the walls of Espíritu Santo in an effort to impact his parishioners' lives. That he had previously rescued Miguel, his odd-jobs man at the church, from a life of poverty in exchange for a place to sleep had seemed the ultimate in social justice. The world outside frightened Pedro. Maybe Alberto was right. Why get involved? Was it worth the danger?

Miguel was sweeping up the church after Mass when two soldiers entered the sanctuary. They eyed him up and down. "We're looking for Father Villanueva," one of the soldiers said.

"Do you have an appointment?" asked Miguel.

"We don't need an appointment! Now are you going to get him, or do we have to do it ourselves?" The soldiers unbuckled the snaps of the leather flaps covering their holstered pistols.

"I'm not sure where he is, but I'll go look, señores. Just a moment." Miguel disappeared behind the altar and headed to Pedro's office.

"What do they want?" Pedro asked.

"They didn't say, Father," he said. "I think maybe you should leave through the back door, and I'll tell them I couldn't find you."

"That's tempting, but no sense putting off unpleasant things. They don't get better on their own. Tell them to come back here."

"But, Father—"

Pedro held up his index finger. "Go get them. Now!" he ordered.

Miguel escorted the soldiers to Pedro; they explained that they'd been asked to bring him to La Cabaña. Pedro felt his heart pulsating. Had someone found out he was trying to free Homero from prison?

"What's this about?" Pedro demanded, hoping he sounded authoritative.

"We just follow orders, Father. I'm sure the captain will tell you when you get there."

There was no choice but to accompany the soldiers.

Pedro felt some hope—no one had made any motion to handcuff him.

They rode to the fortress in silence. On the eastern shore of Havana Bay, La Cabaña was a massive stone battlement, approachable from the street by crossing over a drawbridge. Pedro passed through the gaping hole in the prison wall that formed the entrance, past khaki-clad soldiers with steel helmets. His footsteps echoed down the narrow corridor, and the low brick ceiling hung heavily overhead. Despite the thickness of the walls, the prison was hot, and Pedro's cassock was soon soaked with perspiration.

Passing through two twenty-foot iron gates, he arrived at a paved yard that stank of urine. To his right, he saw that the white-painted stone wall was bullet scarred. Red stains on the ground suggested the executions that must have taken place there. In the distance loomed a square cellblock. Arrow-slit windows peered out from the top of the walls.

Pedro was led inside among rows of cells constructed of rusty bars that resembled cages for animals. Each cage was no more than six feet wide and about ten feet in length. Without running water and only a bucket for waste, it appeared that in this zoo, the animals weren't cared for; they were tortured. He was brought before the soldiers' commander, Captain Emilio Alvárez, who had a pockmarked face and a weak smile. The captain shook Pedro's hand limply and picked up a file.

"We have this prisoner, Carlos Mangas, who's scheduled to be executed in the morning. He's asked for a priest—you, in particular. Any idea why he'd choose you?"

Immediately Pedro thought, it's Homero. This must be a mistake.

"I don't know the name," said Pedro. "Do you know where he's from? What he did?"

"The only thing I have on him is that he was one of those Echeverria hooligans who protested against the closure of the university and tried to kill our president."

Pedro didn't react, but a great sense of injustice overcame him. Too bad they failed, he thought.

Two guards escorted Pedro to the cage of a young man whose face had been beaten so badly that dried blood sealed his left eye closed. He was propped up against the far corner of the cell, his nose broken and his right arm hanging limply to the side. Pedro couldn't understand how he could still be alive. The cage reeked of urine and feces, and Pedro gagged involuntarily.

"My son, you asked for a priest," said Pedro soothingly. The only movement was that of shallow breathing. Pedro knelt on one knee and gently shook the prisoner's shoulder. The man moaned quietly. "Carlos, can you hear me?" Pedro asked.

Behind him, Pedro could hear the guards snickering to each other. Pedro stood up and faced them. "There's nothing funny going on here. Leave me alone with the prisoner. Get out!"

34

The guards blanched. "Father, our orders are to stay with you to protect you," one of them said.

"Do I look like I'm in any danger?" asked Pedro sternly.

The guards backed away. Pedro made the sign of the cross and took the prisoner's hand. He opened his one good eye. "Father, it's me."

"Do I know you, my son?"

"Havana Yacht Club." The boy formed the words in a tortured effort to make himself heard. He coughed, and bloody spittle drooled from the corner of his mouth. He whispered a final word: "Busboy," and lost consciousness.

Pedro gasped. In horror, he remembered—this poor soul had been arrested the night he'd first met Dolores Barré after the Lightning regatta.

Why did he ask for me? Pedro wondered. He didn't remember ever having spoken to him. He had no recollection of ever having seen him at Espíritu Santo. Pedro looked at the brutally battered body. There was nothing he could do for him, except to administer last rites.

Pedro could not exorcise the image of the tortured busboy. As he left the prison, for the first time he realized that he needed to do something, anything, to help such victims of social injustice. Somehow he had to not only free Homero, but also do more to help end this bestial display of authority.

His unhappiness at being a priest no longer seemed important at all; existing from day to day under the

35

radar was no longer enough. The mangled face of the busboy was a call to action. He shook his fist at the sky. "*Non serviam!*" he yelled. "You've deserted us! You've abandoned me! There is only me and I will not be quiet!"

Chapter 5

The next Sunday, Pedro looked out on his congregation and sadly noted that the church still had many empty pews. However, at the end of one of the pews near the rear sat the apparition from the Havana Yacht Club. Even with her hair hidden by a modest black mantilla, there was no mistaking her. It was Dolores Barré. Since the night of the Lightning regatta, he had thought often of Dolores's sensuous dancing in her red dress. That he could immediately see her was a painful reminder of his conversations with Domingo. His congregants once more had voted with their feet on the question of the quality of his production. Clearly, I am a miserable showman, he thought. When he realized he was staring at her, he looked away, not only to divert the few congregants' attention but, more importantly, to cover his own shame at lusting after Dolores when he had recently resolved to devote himself to fighting for social justice.

The services went as usual—with many yawns, and one rotund woman, her head bobbing against her chest, snoring. Flora Olivos sat in the middle of the congregation sobbing with her daughter, Lola. Whispers buzzed throughout the Mass, as parishioners sought an explanation for the disturbance. Pedro stood at the lectern to give his homily and waited for silence. He wanted to say something to bring Flora comfort and to inspire the others, particularly Dolores, the one congregant he wished to impress.

Pedro began to speak, his voice tremulous. "Ordinarily, I would now comment on today's message about the calling of Matthew." Pedro steadied himself, gripping the altar with his left hand. He continued, "That's what priests are supposed to do after reading the daily gospel. But judging by your faces and the murmurs that have filled our sanctuary this morning, I know that you have more pressing concerns than what Matthew has to teach us."

A few congregants nodded in agreement. Lola Olivos buried her face in her mother's bosom and moaned.

Pedro held up the notes for his sermon and ripped them in half.

"It isn't the policy of our church to get involved in politics," Pedro declared. He paused for effect. "As your priest, I am to teach the words of the Gospel. That's what you have heard me do every time I've stood on this pulpit, and that's what I was prepared to do this morning. However, as you all apparently know, members of our parish are suffering, without any knowledge of the fate of a loved one who has been ripped from them." He looked at Flora and continued,

"While the church does not involve itself in government, I don't think Saint Matthew will be disturbed if I look elsewhere for guidance this morning."

Pedro could see the look of surprise on the faces of the congregants. Never before had he spoken unscripted.

"Can you imagine what José Martí might say if he were alive today?" He paused to give the congregation time to recall Martí, the most prominent member of the revolutionary movement in Cuba's nineteenth-century struggle for freedom from Spain.

"Do you remember his famous poem, 'A Sincere Man I Am'?"

Pedro felt a lump in his throat as he thought back to his days at Belén School where the Jesuits had pounded Martí's poetry into his memory.

"I have always thought that the fourth stanza is particularly comforting in times like these. Martí wrote:

> I have seen through dead of night
> Upon my head softly fall,
> Rays formed of the purest light
> From beauty celestial.

"Martí reminds us that even in the bleakest of times, it is imperative to have hope, just as we know that in the darkest, deadest time of night, a time will surely follow when the rays of the rising sun will beautify the heavens."

Flora's sobbing stopped, and she looked up at Pedro in awe.

"So long as we draw breath," Pedro's voice resonated in the sanctuary, "there is hope. So do not despair. There will be light at the end of this trying time."

A few congregants nodded with approval, but others seemed unmoved. He looked to the back of the church, where Dolores was smiling in agreement. Once more, he felt ashamed by the momentary thrill this gave him.

Pedro paused again to give his congregation a few seconds to absorb the first lesson. He cleared his throat and continued, "But Martí teaches us that hope alone is not enough. We must also learn how to deal with those who would oppress us. Do you recall these lines?"

> I cultivate a white rose
> In June as in January
> For the sincere friend
> Who shakes my hand frankly.
> And for the cruel person
> Who would want to break my heart,
> I cultivate, neither thistles nor thorns,
> I cultivate a white rose.

Pedro raised his voice in a final effort to command the congregants' attention and continued, "I hope that in our world in which terrorist bombs go off without warning, and where people seem to disappear from the streets never to be heard from again, we will all remember our higher duty to God and cultivate a white rose for those who would hurt us."

Pedro thought he might have made a point with the majority of his parish. Flora was certainly calmer than before. He looked toward the rear of the church and saw that the smile had vanished from Dolores's face. She did not look pleased.

After the service, Pedro took his station at the front door to greet members of the small congregation as they left. Dolores Barré held back until the last. Today, she was not the coquette he'd observed at the club. She wore a white blouse with three-quarter-length sleeves, a knee-length black skirt as well as the mantilla that covered her head and fell down to her shoulders. Even dressed modestly, she was a knockout. "Not a bad sermon for a sailor, Father," Dolores said.

"I'm glad you liked it. What brings you to my little corner of Havana?"

"God and I aren't speaking to each other, so I don't normally come close to a church. I came today because I find you interesting—a priest who hangs out at swanky clubs. Most of the men I meet at clubs are plutocrats whose only concern seems to be booze and who's screwing whom. I've been meaning to come to hear you sooner, but I've been busy with other things. I don't agree with everything you said, but you might finally be a priest I can talk to. I have some things on my mind."

"My door is always open to the flock."

"Fuck the flock!" Dolores watched Pedro carefully, as if to gauge the effect of her words.

41

"My child, we're not at the Havana Yacht Club. We at the church are not ready for your salty language, I'm afraid." Pedro chastised her with a smile.

"Okay, I'll get serious. I do need to talk to you, Father, so I'll call you during the week." She removed her mantilla and hurried away gracefully, almost dancing. The fragrance of her perfume still lingered in Pedro's nostrils long after she'd disappeared.

During the next several days, Pedro thought less of his vows to help the oppressed and more of Dolores, and every time the phone rang he was disappointed when the answer to his hello was usually from his mother. "Fuck the flock" reverberated through his consciousness. He knew Dolores had wanted to shock him and, unaccountably, he didn't care.

Finally, she called, sounding hurried. No pleasantries, no homage to polite chitchat. "Meet me at the club where we first met," she said tersely.

Pedro started to say the club's name.

"No names," she said. "I'm not on a private line. And who knows who's listening on your end. I'll be there at two P.M. If there's a problem, here's my number." She hung up without so much as a "See you later." Pedro's phone went dead. He wrote down the number she'd dictated.

What to make of the truncated call? Eavesdropping? Pedro couldn't imagine that someone would be interested in *his* telephone calls, let alone be concerned with women's gossip. It was like something out of a movie.

As he washed up, he turned on the radio to hear the latest news of the Havana Sugar Kings, his favorite minor-league team. The announcer was running down the scores of the National League when the station shifted coverage to the news desk:

THIS IS RADIO AEROPUERTO INTERNACIONAL, THE VOICE OF MAJOR-LEAGUE BASEBALL, RE-PORTING THAT A CEASEFIRE IN THE WAR HAS BEEN ANNOUNCED BY FIDEL CASTRO. PRESIDENT BATISTA'S OPERATION VERANO HAS RESULTED IN MASSIVE CASUALTIES TO THE REVOLUTIONARIES. CASTRO'S REQUESTED NEGOTIATIONS ARE UN-DERWAY FOR A SETTLEMENT OF THE WAR...

Pedro set out for the club in his old Plymouth Deluxe. His father called it the "teal monster" when he gave him the keys after graduation from the University of Havana. Its once perfect paint had succumbed to the sea air, and the fender shields around the rear tires had started to rust. Dolores, in the entryway by the main door, where guests were required to wait for a member to accompany them into the club, was not at all mysterious. Part of him was deflated, as she'd seemed so thick with intrigue. Pedro led her to the bar.

Over lunch, Dolores was full of news about the latest doyenne of Havana society suspected of having an affair with a government minister. As she prattled on about one inconsequential subject after another, Pedro wondered why there'd been such urgency to meet. He focused on his last morsels of ceviche and waited. He'd discovered in conversations with his mother that often what was most important to Asunción came last. All else was prelude. Perhaps all women were like that.

Sure enough, as the busboy brought coffee, Dolores let him have it. "Will I go to hell if I get married outside the church?"

"There are many roads to hell," Pedro replied as coolly as possible in his startled state. "Just as there are many roads to God."

"I don't believe in God."

"Then why are you worried about going to hell?"

"I was brought up to believe that the goal of every girl should be to marry in a church. In Santiago, where I was born, every girl dreams of a church wedding with white gladiolas, rice, and candles."

"Who's the lucky man?"

"You can't tell anyone, promise?" Dolores looked around the bar, checking to see if anyone was watching.

"What you tell me has the sanctity of the confessional."

"Luis," she whispered.

"Luis?" Pedro asked. "Luis who?"

"Father, please lower your voice—there is only one Luis." She looked Pedro in the eyes and added, "Ferrer."

Pedro blanched. "You're planning on marrying

44

Fidel's top *comandante*? How is that possible? He's up in the mountains, fighting in this endless revolution."

"You're wrong, Father. Our revolution *will* have an end, and the days until then are numbered."

"Our revolution? You mean you're part of these so-called freedom fighters? My God!"

None of his fantasies about Dolores had foretold this. What would she say next?

"We learn from our mistakes, like in the general strike that fizzled. We won't make that mistake again," Dolores said proudly. "And Batista is losing his grip. Soon this will all be over."

"I'm not so sure," Pedro replied. "Radio Aeropuerto Nacional has just broadcast news about the battle at La Plata. Fidel has asked for a ceasefire that was granted, and they're now talking about having a negotiated settlement of the war."

"Don't believe everything you hear on the radio," advised Dolores.

"If you say so. I'm just a priest, and the Church stays out of politics. As for hell, I'm no expert. But if you marry him in a church, what have you got to lose? If you don't get married within the church and you die and there is no hell, are you any better off for having violated the teachings of our faith?"

"Father, this is exasperating. What you're really telling me is that you don't have an answer to my question."

"I didn't say that. If it's the church—wonderful! If it isn't, then I'm not one to argue with your choice. Live

45

a life of purpose. That's my only advice. We live in a broken world—repair it."

Hypocrite, Pedro thought to himself.

"I think I'm doing that, although sometimes you have to destroy before you build again. Some things cannot be repaired." Dolores sat back in her chair and caught Pedro's eye. "It's easy to talk to you," she murmured.

"Call anytime, day or night. My church never sleeps." Pedro thought he sounded like an ad for a delivery service. "In fact, it's time for me to scoot back there. The roof over my office is leaking, and if I don't supervise, my desk will float away the next time a hurricane blows in."

"Let me leave first, Father," said Dolores. "I'm not sure it's so safe for you to be seen with me on the street. You should know that I'm a messenger to the revolutionaries in the mountains. Luis, Raúl, Fidel, Camilo, Che. I bring them medicine and bandages. There are spies everywhere."

Pedro was somewhat stunned that she was being so open about her clandestine activities but, after all, he *had* promised that any information she shared would stay with him.

"I didn't see a soul when I came in. Don't you think you're being a little paranoid?" he asked.

"When you've been doing this for as long as I have, you learn to be careful."

There was no point in arguing. The only other diners in the bar during lunch were two men puffing on cigars. Dolores got up and walked past them, but they didn't even glance at her. Pedro followed her with his eyes until the door of the bar closed.

What am I doing here? he asked himself. A fine example of a priest I am—obsessed with this woman's dancing, her bikini. And she's the one worried about going to hell?

Pedro left five minutes later and walked to his Plymouth. He noticed that both cigar smokers were now at the entrance of the club. One of them had a notepad. As Pedro drove away, he saw the man staring at the back of his Plymouth and scrawling hurriedly. In 1958 Havana, one could never be absolutely sure of anything.

Chapter 6

Several weeks later, still in his cassock after a Tuesday-morning Mass, Pedro was at his desk puzzling over a homily he'd hoped might be *the* message that would demonstrate anew some guidance to his parishioners. Writing was always a struggle for him. He stared at a blank page, but words failed him. Whatever he put on paper he thought simplistic and hardly worth the effort of distilling something usable. Writing an entire true sentence seemed unattainable.

Pedro balled up his latest effort and tossed it under his desk. He wasn't sure if he simply didn't know anything important or whether he just lacked focus. As he tried to organize his thoughts, his mind darted among fragmentary visions of his visit to La Cabaña, his mother's entreaties for him to become a priest, and his recent lunch with Dolores. Feet up on his desk, he leaned back in his chair. As he crushed still another sheet of paper, the phone rang. He stared at it blankly. The phone rang again. He wasn't getting anywhere with his sermon, so he reached for the handset. When he heard Dolores's sultry voice, he sat up straight, at attention.

"Father," Dolores began, "you remember the work that I do up in the mountains?"

"Do you think I could ever forget that? You have no idea how that conversation shattered my image of you." Pedro wondered if she could hear the quiver in his voice.

"I need some help, and I don't know who to call. It's about your father—"

"My father?"

"I remember that he's a doctor. Your brother introduced us."

"Are you ill?"

"No, it's not me. But I can't talk about this on the phone. I'm at a café in El Vedado. I need to see you right now."

Pedro didn't hesitate. He took down the address and bounded for his old Plymouth. Dolores was only three and a half miles from Espíritu Santo, but the normally fifteen-minute drive ground to a halt at an intersection where a hearse adorned with *coronas de flores* led a long line of black limousines and automobiles snaking toward a cemetery.

Judging by the number of vehicles involved, it must be a baseball player on his final trip to the Necrópolis Cristóbal Colón, Pedro thought. They like to bury the big shots there. He nodded to himself and made a sign of the cross, impatiently drummed his fingers on the steering wheel. As the last of the procession finally cleared the intersection, he shifted into first gear and gunned the engine, burning rubber as the Plymouth lurched forward.

El Vedado was swank and the site of the grandest of the new hotels—the Hilton and the Riviera. Its streets were lined with smart shops and clubs that catered to tourists. The Malecón, a walk running for miles along its ocean seawall, was Havana's social hub and ocean breakwater, and formed one of the area's boundaries. He found Dolores waiting at the entrance to the café. Gone were both the sexy evening dress and the demure mantilla. Instead, she wore dark slacks and a long-sleeved shirt. Her hair was up and covered with a baseball cap. She looked like a young man.

"So who needs a doctor?" Pedro asked the moment they were seated.

"It's a friend. My *camarada* Jorge and I were delivering a load of guns to the rebels at a farmhouse about fifty miles west of Camagüey. A platoon of Batista's bastards came out of nowhere, and there was a fire fight. We wiped them out, but Jorge was shot in the leg. I drove all night with Jorge hidden in the back of the truck. He's in bad shape and bleeding. That's why I thought of your father."

"Guns? You told me you took medicine and bandages. That's a far cry from firefights and gunrunning. Holy Mother of G—"

"I told you what you needed to know," Dolores interrupted. "I'm sorry, but it's hard to know who to trust."

"But you don't understand. My father is an ob-gyn,

not an emergency-room doctor. Why don't you just go to the hospital?"

"If I do that, we'll both end up in La Cabaña!"

Pedro flashed back to his visit and thought of Homero wallowing there still. He couldn't allow a woman to get within miles of that cesspool.

"I've hidden my friend inside Necrópolis Cristóbal Colón in one of the mausoleums, and I need to bring a doctor to him. Is your father *for* the revolution?"

"He's for saving people's lives. He's not involved in politics."

"But, we have to—"

"There's no time to talk," Pedro interrupted. "I'll see my father."

"How the hell did you get messed up with the revolutionaries?" Dr. Hugo Villanueva demanded of his son as they inched through the streets of Havana in Hugo's brand-new Cadillac. It was midday, and traffic was slow going through the heat. Fortunately, the car was air-conditioned, unlike Pedro's old Plymouth, and he would have enjoyed the ride but for the stress of the moment.

"I knew that girl was trouble the moment I saw her on the dance floor!"

"Yes, I know, Father. But we can't let Batista send another victim to La Cabaña, and we have to help her friend who's been shot. I've been to that place, and it's inhuman what goes on there. You don't want to know."

Hugo parked his car near the gate of Necrópolis

Cristóbal Colón. Dolores was waiting inside the entrance and quickly led them past a white marble statue of Mary Magdalene ministering to a lifeless body of Christ to a small mausoleum. It was still under construction and had not yet been given its marble façade to blend with the more than five hundred other mausoleums of this city of death. Inside, a middle-aged man in a sleeveless undershirt was lying on the ground. Blood seeped through a loose tourniquet that wrapped his thigh. Pedro's father went to work, while Dolores and Pedro watched.

"Will he be all right?" Dolores asked.

"He's lost quite a bit of blood, but the bullet went clear through. I cleaned and stitched him and put some sulfa powder on the wounds. What he needs now is rest." Hugo handed an envelope of sulfa to Dolores. "For when you change his bandages each day."

Hugo turned to his son. "Now let's get the hell out of here. We've done what we can."

"You go, Papá. I'll help Dolores get him someplace safe."

Hugo's face reddened. "You don't know what the hell you're getting involved with. You think this is a game? What am I going to say to your mother if you get caught with this guy? Questions are going to be asked, and *you're* the one they'll toss into La Cabaña!"

Pedro stood his ground. "We'll wait with him until evening. When the cemetery empties, we'll get him away from here."

"Are you an idiot?" Hugo asked. "Exactly how are

you planning on getting him out? It's going to be a while until he's walking. Leave him here and come with me to the clinic for a wheelchair. You can push Dolores in the wheelchair up to the mausoleum. Then switch her for my patient. A priest pushing a visitor won't attract attention in this place."

Dolores embraced Hugo in an excited hug. "You've saved Jorge's life. The revolution will be grateful."

Pedro's father looked at her sternly. "Just get my son out of here alive, that's all I ask. And I'll be grateful if I never see you again. And as far as you, my idiot son, your mother expects you for dinner tonight. Don't disappoint her!"

Pedro and Dolores smuggled Jorge from the cemetery into the back of Pedro's Plymouth and hid him on the floor under a blanket. Dolores gave Pedro directions to a house across town. As they were driving, Pedro asked her if they could meet the following day. "I want to learn more about the work you're doing," he explained.

Dolores removed the baseball cap from her head and ran her fingers through her gypsy hair. She no longer looked like a boy.

"Father, I think you've done enough. Why don't you run along to your mother's tonight, as your daddy told you, and forget you saw any of this."

Pedro bristled at her taunt. For the first time in a long while, he felt useful. He didn't want to give that up so easily. "My dear Señorita Barré, after what you

53

put me through today, I think you can spare a little time tomorrow. Meet me around two P.M. at the same café where we met earlier."

Dolores was sitting at a table when Pedro arrived at the café the next afternoon. She wore a lace-trimmed low-cut blouse and a peasant skirt that gave her the Carmen look. When he spoke, he had to fight to look into her eyes rather than into her impressive décolletage.

"You told me that you help gather supplies for the revolution," he said. "I want to know if that's true, or just a story you told me to hide the gunrunning?"

"So?"

"If you're bringing medical supplies and food, I'd like to help. But not guns! I want no part of guns. I've been to La Cabaña, and I've seen things I didn't think possible in modern times."

Dolores gave him a quizzical stare.

"Father, this isn't a picnic. The work is dangerous, as you saw yesterday. People die every day. Sometimes they're just in the wrong place at the wrong time. Sometimes, they deserve it. When we met at your precious club, you didn't seem particularly dedicated to social justice, if you don't mind me saying so. Why now?"

"If not now, when?"

"It's not that we don't need help, Father. But we have to be careful about trusting anyone." She reached over and touched his arm. The gesture felt like a burn.

"You're worried about trusting me after yesterday? I've got no reason to lie. Look, I joined the church to help people. But the only thing I do is hear confessions and mete out penance. Occasionally someone dies and I bury them. Someone marries, I say a Mass. This is not the kind of help I'd hoped to give. I spend most of my time trying to get people to walk in the door of my church."

Pedro realized he was about to step over a threshold into a world where the walls of his church would not confine him, nor would they protect him. He saw the fervor in Dolores's eyes.

"Recently, I saw a man who had been tortured at La Cabaña," Pedro continued. "I could do nothing. The Catholic Church of Cuba says nothing in the face of injustice. It looks the other way. I feel it. I know it. I didn't give my life to the church just to fill the seats on Sunday. I must do more. Maybe you can show me how I can help others from ending up like the poor boy who died in La Cabaña. Yesterday, you gave me hope that I could actually accomplish something."

"You're sure?" she asked quietly. She took his hand. The burning intensified.

"What's sure? I know I can't sleep at night, I'm sure about that. I can't look at myself in the mirror, I'm sure about that. Tell me what I have to do." Pedro leaned back in his chair, shoulders slumped, letting Dolores continue to hold his hand. He felt as if he'd been to confession for the first time in his life.

Dolores ordered beer and a hamburger, but Pedro

had no appetite. "I'm sitting here wondering if I can trust you."

Dolores proceeded to talk with her mouth full. "This is a dangerous business; there are spies everywhere. We can't even trust our friends. Everyone has a price."

"I'm beginning to understand that," Pedro said. "I think I showed you at the cemetery that you can trust me. I'm trying to get the son of parishioners released from La Cabaña right now, and I've learned that even human life has a price."

"A horrible place, La Cabaña. The revolution will put it out of business. When Batista goes, it goes. If you really want to help, then tonight I'll introduce you to our group, the Defarge Circle. Our next shipment to the Sierra Maestra—bandages, tape, sulfa powder, antibiotics, and antiseptic—anything that could be useful to treat injuries in the mountain camps—will be in two weeks. Also, and this is most important, please never use my real name. If you ever have to refer to me, call me Pasionaria."

Dolores scribbled an address of a woman, María Guerra, on a scrap of paper. Pedro knew the area. Pastel-colored houses, many behind garden walls, made up this middle-class suburb. The hilly terrain offered views of distant Havana Bay.

Dolores seemed pleased by Pedro's interest. "Everyone reaches a breaking point with this thug, Batista. He's turned our country into a whorehouse of the Yankees. He tortures our people without mercy. I hope more priests will see that they can't sit on the sidelines; they must use their positions to help the revolution, to return to a real democracy. Now take that paper out of your pocket and memorize the address. Then give it back to me."

Pedro retrieved the creased paper and concentrated on the address: 513 Juan Bruno Zayas, near Carmen in La Víbora. He reflected that his Jesuit education had taught him that Cuba had a long history of failed revolutions. Would Fidel Castro and his brother be any different? He thought back to his school days at Belén and the University of Havana. Fidel had been a classmate. At the time, he'd recognized Castro's brilliance, and his talent as a baseball player. Could he actually succeed where others had failed? He folded the paper and handed it back to Dolores. She struck a match, the paper flared, then turned to ash.

"I don't think I'm a very good priest," Pedro admitted. "I might be a lousy rebel, too."

"You are a man, not a saint, Father. I don't think that either the Golden Rule or the White Rose is satisfying to you. Sometimes, justice must be meted out with a very sharp thorn and not the petals of a wilting rose." Her voice rose with indignation.

Pedro thought Dolores was more intoxicating as a fighter than she'd been on the dance floor. Her sensuality was palpable, and listening to her vehemence made him think that the "calling" for which Father

57

Domingo had told him to listen seemed to be weakening at an accelerated pace. Hearing her repeat the sermon reference about the white rose made him feel more ineffectual than ever. Bribing guards, secret circles, supporting armed revolts—these were not subjects covered at the seminary. Action, that was the ticket.

Chapter 7

Pedro had no trouble finding the address on Juan Bruno Zayas Street. He had served as an assistant nearby at Iglesia de los Pasionistas de la Víbora, a church whose ornate spires seemed dribbled from the hands of a child making a sand castle. As he passed by the church once again, the perfection of its architecture struck him. At the time he'd been an enthusiastic seminary student, going house to house with Brother Ambrosio to raise funds for the church's completion.

He found the house whose address he'd memorized. It was attractive with a red-tiled roof, white stucco walls, and windows curved at their tops in a Moorish style. A walled garden enclosed a fountain in front of the main door. He waited outside for Dolores, impatient that she was late.

"Remember, my name is Pasionaria," she said when she arrived.

Always melodrama, Pedro thought, but went along with her request. Dolores introduced him to their hostess, María Guerra, and the other guests. María and

Pedro chatted until the stragglers arrived. He was impressed by her choice of the latest Danish Modern furniture, but even more taken by a baby grand piano in the corner of the living room.

María, an accountant and third in command at El Tribunal de Cuentas, the Cuban National Tax Collection Agency, resembled a schoolgirl, a contrast to Dolores's earthy sensuality. María introduced him to Juan Gómez, a polo player and engineer who worked for the same firm as her deceased husband. There was Federico, a banker; Enrique, a pharmacist; and Elaina, a dentist—a cross-section of middle- and upper-middle-class Havana society. By the time all of the necessary pleasantries had been observed, the actual business portion of the meeting started almost an hour late.

"I see we're operating on Cuban standard time," María observed. "Revolutions should be run on English time."

Dolores provided a laundry list of items needed by the rebels. When no one volunteered to supply antibiotics, Pedro saw his chance to help.

"I think I can get some sulfa and ampules of penicillin and syringes."

"You, Father? Really?" asked Dolores. "I'd been thinking you might be useful for transportation, what with your expertise with sailboats."

"I could do that, too, I suppose. But you've got a need *now* that I can help with. How do I get the medicine to you?" Pedro's excitement rose. At last, he had a real purpose.

60

"The safest way is for you to put the drugs in your car and then park somewhere. Paseo Street would be a good place—near the corner of Desamparados, by the Malecón. To allow enough time for the next person in the chain to get them from the car, take a walk for an hour. That way, if the police pick up either of you, neither will ever be able to identify the other. Leave the car unlocked and keep the penicillin and sulfa and the syringes in the trunk. Put the trunk key under the floor mat of the front passenger seat."

She's been doing this a while, Pedro thought. Beautiful, smart, *and* cunning.

"When do you need this done?"

"The day after tomorrow."

"That shouldn't be a problem. I'll leave the car there at two o'clock."

"Where are you going to get the drugs?"

"The same place I recently found some help for your wounded friend."

"I noticed your helper wasn't too happy when he left."

"You let me worry about the supply," Pedro said with a certainty he didn't feel inside. "He'll do what he can to make sure someone who needs drugs gets them, whether it's for a Fidelista or a Batistiano."

Pedro was relieved that no one in the Defarge Circle was curious about the identity of his drug source.

"I think you'd better dress in civilian clothes, Father," said María. "You'll attract less attention."

"That's probably a good idea," echoed Dolores. "It

would be even better if you went with a woman. There's a restaurant down the street. At two o'clock it would be the perfect time for a lunch date. María, are you game?"

The meeting was interrupted by María's three children bursting into the library, giggling and chasing each other. The members of the circle greeted them cordially, except for Dolores, who glared at the upstarts. María quieted them down immediately and presented each to Pedro. Roberto, the oldest, was fifteen, Reneé was twelve, and Ruby, ten. "Now, off with you. I'm sure you have homework to do. How did your grandmother let you get down here?"

"She fell asleep." Ruby laughed. "And we escaped!"

"We'll talk about this later. Now, *váyanse!*"

Pedro admired the way María's blue eyes twinkled as she disciplined her children.

María turned back to the meeting as her kids stomped out. "You know that field operations make me nervous," María demurred.

"Come on chiquita, you've got to show some cojones," Dolores shot back. "Shit! I'd do it myself, but I'm going to Santiago de Cuba after this meeting,"

"They watch me like a hawk at work," said María.

"For Christ's sake, we're only talking about lunch!" Dolores demanded. "You do eat, don't you?"

Pedro looked around the room. If he were to be having a lunch date, María suddenly seemed a more desirable candidate than Dolores.

"María, you'll be off the street before anyone knows you've left your building."

María smiled at Pedro. "Okay, Father, you win. But I must be back at El Tribunal by four o'clock." Pedro noted how gently she spoke compared to Dolores's bossiness, and how easily a smile came to her face.

The conspirators finished their meeting-making plans for their next encounter while entertaining some ongoing doubts. "Pasionaria, are we really bringing about real change?" asked María hesitatingly.

"This revolution is not going to be won in one dramatic victory, it's going to be won a little bit each day," Dolores replied, leaning forward in her chair and pointing a finger at each participant. "It's being fought in living rooms and boardrooms, in the streets and in the jungle. Tonight's meeting is just another small step toward the eventual fall of Batista."

Pedro felt he had never witnessed so much commitment. In his church, every custom, every rule, seemed old and stale. Here, they're inventing the rules as they go along, he thought.

"Just remember," Dolores continued, "Fidel started with only thirteen men."

Pedro remembered the news accounts of the arrival of the *Granma*, the old boat on which Fidel and eighty-two rebels left Mexico in 1956 to take up the revolution in the Sierra Maestra. Only thirteen had made it to the mountains.

Dolores concluded, "From that small number, the

revolution has grown into the thousands. It needs the support that's only available in cities such as Havana and Santiago. Eventually, we'll win. I don't know when that will be, but I believe it will be soon."

"I hope to God you're right," said Pedro.

"I put my faith in Fidel, Luis and Raúl—not God." Dolores replied.

Pedro was back at his desk planning his weekly homily the next evening. It was close to 8:45 P.M., and the church was silent and somewhat comfortable. Unlike the new buildings springing up all over Havana, Pedro's church office had no air-conditioning. The church's thick stone walls were insulating, and the arrival of a recent gift from his mother—an oscillating General Electric fan whose constant whirr provided a cooling breeze—was even more helpful.

During daylight hours, with congregants intermittently stopping in to discuss a wedding or a funeral, it was difficult for Pedro to concentrate. The evening brought distractions of a different kind that he couldn't blame on anyone else. His thoughts were a jumble of images of La Cabaña, Dolores, the Defarge Circle, Jorge, his father, María.

Although he'd only met Maria Guerra once, she'd made an impression as lasting as Dolore Barré's. Her beauty was softer than Dolores's. He could tell from the warmth she displayed when she'd playfully dismissed her children that she was a loving mother. She must be pretty smart, too, being part of the top echelon at El Tribunal de Cuentas.

As for his father—he was going to be a challenge. At the cemetery, Pedro had pushed him to the limit. He would give Dr. Hugo a little more time before asking him for medicines for the rebels. But no sooner had he dismissed his father from his thoughts than Homero, still incarcerated in La Cabaña, popped into his mind. What was Alberto up to? He said he'd help. Was Homero even still alive? That poor busboy—was Homero going to end up the same way?

Pedro forced himself back to his sermon. La Cabaña was fertile ground for fresh ideas with which to confront his congregants. Fashioning a moral response to evil and man's inhumanity to man was a compelling topic for priestly advice. At last, he became so focused on his writing that he failed to notice that Alberto had come into his office, accompanied by their older brother, Tomás. Finally, maybe some action!

"To what do I owe the honor of my two brothers coming into the sacred world of Espíritu Santo?" Pedro asked formally. "I cannot imagine that you two have come to confess."

"Very funny," muttered Tomás.

To Pedro's knowledge, Tomás hadn't been to church since Pedro had been ordained as a priest five years earlier.

"I didn't think the world of medicine was about to enter into the spiritual realm," responded Pedro.

"Hey, you two, be cool," said Alberto. "We didn't come here for religious debate."

"And yet you're here for something," said Pedro. "What's up?"

"I mentioned your little problem to our dear brother here."

"Homero is not such a little problem," sighed Pedro.

"If it can be fixed with money, it *is* a little problem," said Tomás. "I see women with problems every day that no amount of money can fix."

"Yes, but to Homero's family, five thousand dollars is a fortune and a *big* problem," said Pedro.

"Luckily, for them, their priest is well connected," replied Tomás. "I've taken the liberty of speaking to a few doctors in the hospital, and they've all agreed to make a little donation to your beautiful church. Alberto and I contributed a few pesos of our own."

Tomás reached into his jacket pocket and handed an envelope to Pedro. "I noticed that this place needs some painting."

Pedro opened the envelope. Inside were fifty 100 hundred dollar bills. "I can buy a lot of paint with this," Pedro said, nodding slowly.

Tomás smiled. "That's up to you, Father."

Pedro embraced his brothers. They might love money and prestige, but family came first. In the distance, a giant roar shook the office. Pedro glanced at his watch. It was nine P.M. La Cabaña's cannon was once again signaling its nightly salute.

Chapter 8

Summer's end approached, and the hurricane season was in full attack. The fifth tropical storm of the year morphed into Hurricane Ella and struck Santiago de Cuba with a vengeance on September 2, 1958. A category-three storm, it flooded the city. Havana avoided the brunt of the wind's fury, but the drenching rains drove citizens to contemplate their existence.

The storm mirrored the turmoil that Pedro had brought on himself when he'd volunteered to get penicillin for Dolores. Despite his glowing description of his father's love of humanity, he considered the possibility of dodging the explanations and breaking into his father's clinic to steal what he needed. Almost as quickly as he had that thought, he realized that he would have to ask—there was no shortcut.

While Pedro had always revered his father, Dr. Hugo Villanueva was a formidable man. He was committed to the physical health of his patients, period. He had never publicly or privately advocated for or against Fidel Castro. At least Pedro had never heard a word about it from him. Among his patients were the wives of many of the highest-ranking officials in the Batista government. Still, he also volunteered at a free clinic one afternoon a week, providing gynecological services for poor women.

Pedro mustered all his courage to beard the lion in his den.

Dr. Hugo's medical office was located in central downtown Havana in a single-story clinic of white stucco. At one end of the building, a second level housed supplies and medications, and access was controlled by an iron gate. There was no air-conditioning, but ceiling fans kept a steady warm breeze blowing. Everywhere, the air smelled of antiseptic. Pedro parked to the side of the building and walked past a line of palm trees standing like sentinels along the approach to the entry.

His father was just leaving an examining room when Pedro walked into the lobby. Pedro noted that his father was graying at the temples, but it only served to make him look more distinguished. His light complexion revealed a few age spots here and there.

"Aha, it's my son the Father!" Hugo exclaimed. "No roller skates today, eh?" As a child, Pedro had loved roller-skating across the shiny floors, although a stern nurse often cut short his escapades on wheels. But Dr. Hugo was less concerned with noisy children than he was with fighting disease, and never disciplined Pedro about the skating.

"No, sorry to disappoint you." Pedro smiled, remembering his boyhood skates. "Best I can do for excitement now is cycling on the Malecón."

"What brings you here today?" his father asked.

His voice subdued as if he were in church uttering a prayer, Pedro said, "Papá, I need to speak to you about a very private matter."

Hugo put his arm around his son's shoulders and walked him down the hallway to a private office.

"So tell me, what's so hush-hush?" Hugo took a seat behind the desk and gestured for his son to sit down in the chair opposite.

"I am helping the Fidelistas in the revolution," Pedro blurted out.

"You're doing what?" Dr. Hugo started up from his chair. "Are you suffering from heat stroke? I thought I made myself clear at the cemetery with that hussy Dolores. You've got a secure job at a historic church, and you want to become a revolutionary?"

"That's not what I said. I simply want to help their cause," Pedro explained.

"Your mother's going to go over the edge. What exactly does 'helping the Fidelistas' mean?"

"Fidel and the others are completely dependent on getting supplies from the cities. In particular, they need antibiotics."

"I can understand that," his father allowed cautiously. "There's a lot going on in the Sierra Maestra that is hazardous to the health. You saw it yourself with that Jorge."

"There's a group here that meets at—"

Hugo held up his hand. "Don't tell me. Please don't tell me. What I don't know, I can't say."

"Well, I promised the leader of the group that I could get penicillin."

If I mention Dolores's name again, Pedro thought, he's going to really let me have it.

"And you thought you could just waltz in here and bat your eyes at me, and I would give you some?"

"I didn't think about batting my eyes, but yes, I thought you might just give me some. They may be revolutionaries, but they are still human beings."

"With their scraggy beards, they look more like apes. I guess that's why they call them guerrillas?"

Pedro smiled wanly.

His father stood up and came around the desk. He placed a hand on Pedro's shoulder. "How much do you need?" Dr. Hugo asked reluctantly.

"I'm not sure. How much can you give?" asked Pedro.

Hesitatingly, he began his story about his recent experience at La Cabaña. "I cannot sit idly by while they commit these acts."

"What does the archdiocese have to say about this?"

"The archdiocese is as silent as the statue of Jesus on the altar at Iglesia del Espíritu Santo. The archbishop only worries about church attendance and hasn't lifted a finger to help Fidel or solve the problem of Batista's corruption."

"You've been a priest for five years, and if you don't

mind my saying so, you sound like you're just tired."
Dr. Hugo gave his youngest a concerned look.

"There's a lot to being a priest that I no longer like.
In fact, I'm not sure I ever liked the things I have to do.
I see suffering all around, and I don't seem able to do
anything to help."

"That's how I feel a lot of the time," his father acknowledged. He reached up and tousled Pedro's hair.

"Sometimes I think I should have been something
else. I'm not sure that I'm cut out for the life of the
church."

His father stepped away and began to pace the floor
in the small office. "You want to leave the priesthood?
I can't believe you'd hurt your mother like that. Don't
even suggest such a thing. You know how she prayed
for you to be a priest. What's come over you?"

"It's not easy to say, but if I stay in it, it may hurt
me. I—"

"No," Hugo interrupted, slamming his right hand
into his left palm. "I don't want any more talk about
your leaving the priesthood. As far as the revolution is
concerned, I want your assurance that your participa-
tion is going to begin and end with your providing supplies. You're not going to go up there yourself in some
godforsaken Jeep, are you?"

"No, father." Pedro shook his head sadly. He really
wanted to speak more about his life in the church, but
he could see that Hugo had closed the door to that discussion. "I have no plans to go camping in the mountains."

"Batista's a popinjay we could all live without, but we've had worse. It's best not to get involved in politics." Hugo was getting agitated and his voice crescendoed. "Nothing good will come of it." He paused and put his arm around his son. "My concern has always been our family and its happiness. You have two fine brothers who are respected in the community. Your mother is an angel. I only care that the family stays safe and together. There are others who've tried to change Cuba, and they got nowhere but La Cabaña or the grave. As a doctor, I know that once you die, you're dead. Your blessed mother believes in resurrection and the hocus-pocus that your church teaches. I don't. And I want you to be around for a good long time."

"Father, it's only medicine that I'm asking for. It's not like I'm going to go out and shoot someone. I'm just going to be an errand boy."

"That's what you're saying now. But the road you're going down can be very dangerous. You don't know where it's going to lead."

The two men embraced, and Pedro felt tears surfacing.

María Guerra met Pedro on another hot and humid day in downtown Havana. The sun burned like a torch. Pedro was so nervous that the moment María closed the Plymouth's door he took off too fast. The tires squealed and María winced.

"I thought the point was to fade in and not be noticed!" she cautioned.

72

"My mistake," Pedro admitted. "I'm sorry. I've been driving around all morning with contraband penicillin, worrying about getting stopped for inspection. I'll be glad when this little caper is finished."

"I'll be glad when we get someplace cooler. I'm dying in here." María turned the vent window inward so that the breeze hit her directly. "One of the advantages of working in a new high-rise is that we've got air-conditioning."

"Like the rest of the city, I've gotten used to the heat. I try not to think about it."

"Not me. I just got a new Olds, and it's like an icebox on the hottest of days. I can't stand the heat. You're lucky you're not fazed by it." She eyed his guayabera and penny loafers. When they'd met at the Defarge Circle meeting, he'd been wearing his collar and black vestment.

"You look sharp, Father, just like you work in one of these offices," María said, gesturing at the buildings that lined the street. Havana's downtown hummed with commerce, and its white-collar workers scurried about the district looking important.

"Please don't call me 'Father.' I'm just Pedro today, as far as anyone is concerned."

Pedro parked the car, as Dolores had instructed, on a treeless street off the main artery. Canvas awnings over the storefronts provided some protection from the broiling sun. Pedro saw the sign for Las Palmas Café just a hundred yards distant. By its entrance, a beggar woman holding an infant sat on the sidewalk. A straw bowl in front of her held a few pesos. Ignoring her, Pedro and María passed through an archway into a garden lush with ferns. The splash from a large fountain masked most street noises and helped cool the afternoon heat. Brightly colored umbrellas shaded the garden's tables.

The only customers, they took seats under a red umbrella. "This garden is an oasis," said Pedro. "And there aren't many of them in this hot cement-covered city." He removed a handkerchief from his pocket and wiped the sweat from his brow.

"When I'm sailing, it's peaceful and cool just like this. I can forget about what I do the rest of the week. I wonder what life is like in the mountains for those who need our medicine." He scratched at his neck, forgetting that no tight white collar was choking him. He was like any other man today, with an attractive woman by his side.

Their conversation was interrupted by the sound of a police siren, drowning out the splash from the garden's fountain. Pedro thought of his car and wondered if it was connected to the alarming noise. A few seconds passed, and the siren faded in the distance. Whatever emergency there was, it was happening elsewhere. Pedro resumed breathing.

"It's hard to relax in this business," he said. "When I volunteered to help, I wasn't exactly sure what Pasionaria had in mind." Pedro used Dolores's code name, not knowing if María knew Dolores's true identity.

"I hate field work!" said María. "A long time ago, I told Pasionaria that I'd provide a meeting place and take up collections of bandages and food. But smuggling contraband—that's something entirely different. Christ, I've got three children to protect who have no father!"

No sooner had María uttered those words than she blushed. "Sorry, Father, I didn't mean to curse."

"I've heard worse." Pedro reached over and took her hand. "But remember, I'm Pedro—you forgot! Why did you come today if you felt this way?"

"I'm not sure." María took her hand from his and reached for a few *mariquitas* to munch on. "You were new at this and looked a little lost—like a small child on his first day at school."

Pedro was entranced by María's blue eyes and the curly blonde hair that framed her pale face. He recalled the warm softness of her skin for the few seconds he'd held her hand. She was beautiful, but in an entirely different way from the dark and sensual Dolores. Unlike many women who'd given birth to three children, Pedro thought, she had not become matronly, but instead exuded youthful energy.

Her cheeks and neck reddened as he looked at her. "Father—uh, I mean Pedro—you're staring at me!"

Pedro dropped his gaze. "You should always be in a beautiful garden like this."

For Pedro, the lunch hour passed too quickly. María had to return to work, bringing him back to an

75

uncomfortable reality. Make-believe time was over for now, he thought to himself, as he looked one last time at María seated in the garden. He inhaled, taking in a whiff of her perfume that was more intoxicating than the nearby gardenias.

Chapter 9

Saturday night on the Malecón had formerly been a festive time. Families and lovers strolled its four-mile length where the spice of Cuban life could be tasted in its sea air. And when the waves' spray crashed over the seawall, young people laughed as they were soaked. They were more interested in the Afro-Cuban jazz entertaining them by strolling musicians or stealing kisses on "Havana's sofa.

But in the late summer of 1958, it was obvious that the random city bombings had taken their toll, and the usual crowds were gone. There was an air of fear; the few people who came out now moved quickly along, not lingering in lovers' embraces.

It was late night on the last Saturday in September when Alberto and Pedro sped along the streets of the nearly deserted Malecón district to meet the guard from La Cabaña, who was purportedly arranging for Homero's release. Alberto drove his gleaming Cadillac Fleetwood a block past La Cantina del Mar and parked along the curb.

When Pedro and Alberto entered the bar, a few patrons drank at scattered tables. Sad boleros blared from a radio. The smell of beer seemed to have spilled over the years into the very pores of the building. Alberto and Pedro ordered two Cuba Libres.

"Are you sure it's safe here?" Pedro mumbled.

"Stay cool, we'll be fine," Alberto assured him. He patted a revolver tucked in his waistband.

Midnight and there was no sign of either Alberto's contact or Homero. Occasionally, the door opened and one or two customers made their way to stools at the bar. No one looked like off-duty military. The brothers waited until one A.M. and, whispering to Pedro that something was fucked up, Alberto paid their bill.

"Well, that was a colossal waste of time," Pedro complained, stepping out to the street. "What are we—"

Pedro's words were cut off by the sound of tires screeching. A black Ford came to a sudden halt. Four uniformed men got out.

"I believe you have something for me, yes?" asked one of them.

"That's the guy I spoke to," whispered Alberto.

Pedro coughed nervously, but Alberto paid no attention.

"That depends," he said. "Do you have something for *me?*"

"Maybe. Let me see the money."

"Not so fast," Alberto retorted. "Where's the boy?"

"You think I'm trying to cheat you?" sneered the soldier.

Pedro had never admired his calm brother so much.

"My friend, I think you'd steal from your mother," said Alberto. "Now we said we would do a trade. I don't see anything you have to trade with."

The soldier drew his revolver from his holster.

"You don't think I was careless enough to bring five thousand dollars to this part of the world, do you?" asked Alberto. "Use that gun and you'll never see your money." Pedro stepped closer to Alberto.

"You've got some giant cojones, my friend," the soldier laughed. He signaled the other soldiers. "Let's show our lawyer his Christmas present."

One of the soldiers popped the Ford's trunk. They removed a wriggling sack and put it on the street. One pulled open a drawstring, revealing a badly beaten Homero, struggling to extricate himself from the sack. Pedro immediately bent over the young man and helped him to his feet.

"Wh…who…who are you?" asked Homero.

"Don't worry, Homero," Pedro whispered. "We're friends. It's Father Pedro."

Homero's legs started to buckle, and Pedro steadied him. Together, they staggered to the Fleetwood where Alberto waited.

Alberto reached inside his jacket pocket, withdrew an envelope, and threw it to the soldier.

"I thought you said that you didn't have the money on you!" the soldier said. He ripped open the envelope and started counting the bills.

"You never heard a lawyer lie?" Alberto asked. "Let's go, Pedro."

He walked slowly toward his car, cautioning Pedro in a whisper, "Don't turn around." And then, in his professionally assured voice, he said aloud, "That wasn't so bad."

Pedro stood Homero up against the Cadillac's back door. Blood from the boy's cuts and scrapes oozed down the window. Pedro thought in his bewilderment that Alberto wouldn't be happy to see his precious toy sullied. A squeal of rubber as the black Ford accelerated, then screeched to a halt beside the three men — one fumbling with his keys, one propping up the third. A gun barrel pointed out the Ford's right front passenger window, and the windows of Alberto's beloved Fleetwood exploded in a shower of flying glass. A flash erupted from Alberto's handgun. Homero slipped heavily to the ground. Pedro, shielding the boy's body with his own, landed hard on top of him. Hoping that Homero was unhurt by the fall, Pedro got to his feet and gave the boy a tug. Homero staggered toward the front of the Cadillac.

"Oh, Jesus and Mother Mary!" he cried out.

Alberto lay half-in and half-out of the driver's seat, blood pouring over the maroon-and-silver leather seat and down to the floor.

"What have I done to you?" Pedro screamed, as he cradled the lifeless body of his brother in his arms.

Homero crawled away and vomited.

"What should we do?" he asked, panicked.

In the distance, Pedro heard the sounds of a police siren.

"Get out of here now!" he shouted, and pushed Homero away. The boy took off down the darkened street. Pedro laid Alberto's body gently on the bloodied seat and ran to the seawall. With as much strength as he could muster, he threw Alberto's revolver into the ocean. When the police arrived, he was back at the Cadillac, watching over his brother.

Pedro told the authorities that he, Father Pedro Villanueva, and his brother, renowned *abogado* Alberto Villanueva, had been ambushed by armed men in a passing car, but he hadn't been able to get a good look at it or the men. He said that the shooters had fired guns from the front and rear windows. If the police suspected that there was more to the story, they didn't press the investigation.

As for his family, they were another matter altogether. Pedro called Tomás to pick him up from the police station and accompany him to their parents' home to break the terrible news. For once, Pedro paid no attention to the majestic royal palms and bougainvillea gracing his parents' Miramar neighborhood, nor did he stop to savor the scent of jasmine that perfumed the area in all seasons. He was in agony arriving at his childhood home, carrying heavy guilt. At the sight of Pedro's face and bloody clothes, his mother's face turned white, and she sank into the nearest sofa, as if she already knew a tragedy had taken place.

"Alberto's dead," Pedro said, standing in front of his mother, wishing he were anywhere but there.

81

Dr. Hugo appeared in an instant, and without waiting to hear what had happened, slapped his son hard across the face. "I told you that you should mind your own business, and you wouldn't listen!" he cried out, tears pouring down. "Now your brother's dead because of you!"

"Papá, that's not fair!" Tomás shouted, choking back tears himself. "Alberto is dead because he's a hero. He saved a life."

Hugo was not appeased. He blew his nose into his sparkling white handkerchief, trembling with pain and anger.

"If Pedro had kept his faith in the church and his nose out of La Cabaña, Alberto would still be alive." He, too, sank onto the sofa next to his wife.

Asunción had been quiet through the bitter exchange, but now she spoke harshly. "Enough, all of you! Alberto is dead, and none of your shouting is going to bring him back."

Hugo gave his wife an angry dismissal. "An old man should never have to bury one of his children."

Pedro felt like a Cuban *Santero*, being buried himself, bit by bit. He cowered before his father, his face contorted in grief.

"Papá, Papá, forgive me. Blame Alberto's death on me if you wish, but in the name of the Father, forgive my sins." He fell to his knees. "Do you think if I had any inkling this affair would end in Alberto's death, or anyone's, I would have gotten them involved? I'm not a monster. I'm just a weak man!" Through his tears, Pedro was barely coherent.

The funeral took place two days later. That morning, Alberto's body, covered with the red, white, and blue of the Cuban flag, was laid on a bier situated in the living room of his parents' home. Crowds of relatives, friends, members of the Havana bar, and patients of both the Villanueva doctors came to pay their respects.

Asunción and Hugo greeted their visitors from chairs that faced their son's body. Homero approached them cautiously, with an armful of flowers. His face was covered with bruises, and the backs of his hands were black-and-blue. A bandage was taped over one ear.

"Please don't hate me!" he cried, his face contorted with pain. His lips were swollen and his speech was slurred. "He died saving my life. If I rotted another day in La Cabaña, they'd have beaten me to death." He dropped to his knees, putting his head in Asunción's lap.

She ran her fingers through his hair. "He was always such a good boy." She spoke in a tone of despair. "He didn't deserve to die this way."

She sat up, straight and regal. "There's nothing to forgive. He's with God now."

Homero struggled to his feet and stumbled away.

Pedro saw that the unrelenting sadness was making his father very ragged. He'd wished that Hugo had hit him harder—he deserved it. Pedro wondered if his sin could ever be pardoned.

María appeared among the crowd jammed into the Villanueva's home. When she arrived, Pedro was relieved and felt somewhat comforted. She had only seconds to pay her respects to his parents before the press of mourners pushed her aside. Feeling an urgent need to confide in her, he walked her out to the terrace.

"My father hates me for involving my brothers in a boy's escape from La Cabaña. When I asked him for the medicines for Fidel, he lectured me about getting involved politically. And now I've killed my own brother." He bowed his head, whether in sorrow or to prevent her from seeing his tears, he wasn't sure.

María ventured close to him.

"Pedro, that's not true. Batista and his corrupt system killed your brother and will continue to kill more of us until the revolution pushes him into the sea."

"I don't think I can get my parents to understand that. This whole thing makes me sick."

"Give it a little time. They're devastated by grief right now."

Pedro wanted to hug María, to thank her for her assurances, but realized that here, outside his parents' house of mourning, was neither the time nor the place for embracing a woman whom he knew only slightly. He compromised by giving María a brotherly kiss on the cheek.

The funeral at Iglesia del Espíritu Santo later that afternoon filled the church to overflowing. Pedro had done funeral Masses hundreds of times, and he went through today's service like a robot.

But when he began his homily, his voice cracked. "My family has a beautiful sailboat; her name is *La Rosa Blanca*. When I sail out past the protection of Havana Harbor and look around at the sea and the immutable waves, I'm reminded of how it gives me a sense of proportion. The ocean doesn't care that my brother is dead. It doesn't concern itself that my family wails in misery. It doesn't fret if I die today or tomorrow. To some, that means that no one out there cares what happens to us. But I think rather than showing indifference, the sea proves that there's a caring God who has given us a beautiful world full of wonder, but one full of questions whose answers hide beyond the horizon."

Pedro paused. "Out of sight of land, my sailboat is still conquering new waves. However, for the people back on shore, try as they may, they cannot see her."

His audience was still.

"To me, that is what death is like. My brother has gone beyond the horizon, and I cannot see him. I cannot touch him. I cannot hear his loving voice. But just as I know that *La Rosa Blanca* exists when she sails over that horizon, Alberto is there, too—over the horizon, not for us to see any longer, until the resurrection."

After he finished his sermon, the church was dead silent. He had captured the attention of his congregants at last.

Chapter 10

In María's living room, all eight members of the De-farge Circle were present and accounted for.

"I can't believe it—you're all here on time!" Do-lores exclaimed.

The rest of the group glared at María.

"Is there something I should know?" asked Do-lores.

"Well, I have to admit, I played a little trick on you," said María. "I told you to come at seven o'clock. I figured if I did that, we stood a decent chance of start-ing by eight."

"As long as there's a delicious Hungarian finger torte to eat, I'm happy to be tricked," said Enrique. He tore a chunk of cake from its knotted roots and popped it into his mouth. Pedro was very interested to see that revolutionaries liked their food; he had imagined them as ascetics. Domingo would fit in nicely here, he thought.

Dolores's face was animated when she gave them the rundown of battles being fought in the plains. "Che has them shaking in their boots. Won't be long before we march into Havana and stand Batista up against the wall. I saw Che and five comrades wipe out an entire company of the bastards!"

Dolores smiled gleefully. She concluded her instructions with a list of rebel needs: bandages rice, radios, and antibiotics.

Pedro tried to focus, but found his attention wandering. He wondered what Dolores looked like naked.

María began a story about the Hotel Havana Riviera. "That place is run by Meyer Lansky, the American gangster. Our so-called president has made him a minister for tourism." She shook her head in disbelief.

"You know those businesses are exempt from income taxes—they're more of a joint venture with the government—well, we noticed that the Riviera seemed to be losing more than the other casinos, so I sent in a team of auditors."

Pedro turned his attention from undressing Dolores to María's story.

"At first, the private security guards wouldn't let my team in, until Harry Smith, the Canadian president of the hotel, was called to the floor. My boys and I made the cashiers step away from their drawers. A door to an inner office opened, and a guard walked out. Behind him, I spied a desk covered with cash."

María paused to take a breath. "A woman was seated there, shoveling handfuls of dollars into a knitting bag. An expensively dressed man stood next to her. I had seen that particular gentleman in the newspaper when the casino opened—Meyer Lansky in the flesh.

He's ancient; he has wrinkles on his wrinkles! The woman in the chair was no stranger, either—Marta Batista—the wife of the president!"

Pedro thought to himself, So the rumors are true—even the president is on the take!

Dolores rubbed her hands. "We'll get those *coños de sus madres*. Pretty Miss Marta won't look so pretty after a few years in La Cabaña! But listen, María, you have to be careful who you tell stories to. Take nothing for granted. One of my friends is a tailor. He had an assistant who was a police informant. Every day the bastard asked my friend how he felt about the revolution. The tailor told him nothing. One day this asshole pretended he was collecting money for the revolution. To get rid of him, the tailor said that he'd given a donation to Fidel just that very morning. An hour later, he was arrested and thrown into La Cabaña for aiding the revolution. Trust no one, present company *not* excepted."

María blushed. "Of course, you're right. It's best to be discreet," she said, turning toward Dolores. "Particularly, since it's an ongoing investigation. I'm not finished with the folks at that casino yet. Forget I said a word." She turned to look at the others. "But I *do* trust everyone here."

As María apologized, Pedro looked around the room at the members of the Defarge Circle. Could they all be trusted? Was there a traitor here? What about the two women who had just told the circle their stories? He was attracted to both, even though he knew nothing about either.

● ● ●

Several weeks later, at the request of his father, Pedro brought Domingo to visit his mother. She'd been in a dark mood since the funeral—more than a month before—and had spent her days in the house with the shades drawn, refusing to leave for any reason.

"My dear, it's time for you to return to the living," said Domingo consolingly. "It's been more than a month, and I understand you haven't left this house."

"My life is over," Asunción wailed.

"Mother, that's not true," Pedro cried. "We've buried Alberto, not you."

Domingo took a seat next to Asunción and put his arm around her. "Daughter, even when the Holy Father, may God forbid, dies, we mourn only for nine days. The *Novenarios* is our tradition for good reason. Life is precious and it must go on."

Domingo launched into a discussion of food and his favorite cafés. By the time his visit came to an end, he had persuaded Asunción to join Pedro, Hugo, and himself on an outing.

The next evening they were all dazzled by the dream-world of the Havana Riviera Hotel. Passing by a spectacular marble sculpture of an intertwined mermaid and swordfish, into the kaleidoscopic opulence of the lobby, Asunción gasped. She commented that the path to the main restaurant that led them down a promenade surrounded by trees and fountains and across a bridge overlooking sunken gardens reminded her of

89

visiting Disneyland with Hugo two years before. Pedro particularly enjoyed the scent of flowers that perfumed the air. It reminded him of María.

Pedro watched his mother carefully. At first she seemed very reserved and unsmiling, but as deferential waiters balanced trays of rainbow-colored frozen drinks and waved flaming kebobs like bullfighters in the ring, she became caught up in the frivolity. When a flaming baked Alaska was set down in front of her, she almost looked happy. After dinner, Dr. Hugo puffed on a cigar, while drinking coffee and Courvoisier with Pedro and Domingo. Pedro breathed a sigh of relief. Sniffing the woody fumes of his cognac, he finally relaxed. And then, María walked toward him followed by three men. This evening's fantasy was complete.

"Father, what a pleasant surprise!" she said

"Aren't you going to introduce me to this lovely lady?" asked Domingo, tearing himself away from his second portion of baked Alaska. He pounded his ample abdomen gently. "I'm not exactly invisible, you know."

Pedro introduced Domingo to María as a member of his parish, and she returned the introduction with a furtive wink.

"I'm here working tonight, I'm afraid," she announced, and explained that she was chief of auditing for El Tribunal de Cuentas.

"You're the most beautiful tax man I've ever met," said Hugo. "Makes me want to pay more taxes. And what brings the chief auditor out on such a beautiful night?"

"We're doing an audit of the casino."

Pedro tried to change the subject.

"Father, don't worry," María interrupted. "The government is a partner in the profits of the hotel. However Mr. Lansky conducts himself in the United States, I can say with some authority that his dealings in Cuba are legitimate. Perhaps too much so."

She paused. "This casino doesn't make as much money as the others." María shot a glance at Pedro, her eyes twinkling mischievously. Careful, careful, Pedro thought to himself.

"You see," said Domingo, "there are miracles—even the crooks have become honest."

Pedro was glad to see that Domingo's joke brought a small chuckle from his mother. As he watched María's easy, friendly way with his parents, he remembered the warmth of her touch at lunch and began to concoct another excuse to be with her.

The next few days gave Pedro more time to think about María. He had no jobs to do for the Defarge Circle, and his work at the church was mind numbing. He sat at his desk and stared at the phone. He picked it up and started to dial, then slammed down the receiver. What's wrong with me? he asked himself. He went to the window looking out on the streets of Old Havana. A man strolled down the street, his arm embracing a woman whose head rested on his shoulder. Pedro reached up and pulled at his white collar with annoyance. In the heat of the Havana afternoon, it chafed.

He picked up the phone once again and dialed. María answered on the first ring.

"Father, is there something in particular you wanted?"

It was now or never. "I...I was hoping that we might meet. I have some concerns about the...group."

"Oh, you mean the cir—"

"Not on the phone," he interrupted.

"Well then, where?"

"I have a boat. Actually, it's my father's, but I'm the only one in the family who ever uses her. Perhaps you can meet me on Saturday at the Havana Yacht Club—that's where she's moored."

"Sailing? Me?"

"There's no better place for a private conversation."

Pedro waited for her answer. The seconds felt like hours.

"What time?" she asked, as if meeting him was the most natural thing in the world.

Pedro didn't sleep the night before the sail. It was only when he spied *La Rosa Blanca* bobbing at her mooring, the sun glistening off her mahogany hull and teak deck, that he felt fully awake. His father had purchased her from a yacht broker in Amsterdam. Pedro remembered that when she'd arrived, he'd been ten, and the whole family had piled into the car and had gone to the shipyard to see her off-loaded from the freighter.

Pedro inspected below deck and opened the portholes to allow the sea breeze to refresh the cabin. Stowing away a lunch he'd carefully packed, he checked his watch—another half-hour. The wait felt interminable. Fortunately, María arrived ten minutes early, relieving him of his misery.

First, Pedro showed off the boat—how to attach the halyard to the head of the mainsail and then hoist it, how the galley's stove worked, how small but snug the fore and aft cabins were. Finally, *La Rosa Blanca* slipped away from her dock and out to the open water. Before long, La Cabaña faded to a small shadow on the distant shore. María, clad in shorts and a peasant blouse, stretched out on the cockpit's cushions and covered her long legs with Coppertone oil. Pedro felt he had never seen such a beautiful sight.

"Can I steer?" María asked.

"Well, certainly, just put your hands—both of them—on the wheel here," said Pedro.

He stood behind her and guided her hands into position. *La Rosa Blanca* responded by turning slightly to starboard. María was getting the hang of holding a steady course and that pleased Pedro. She was a good learner.

"I can see why you like to sail—this is amazing. My kids would love this."

"You won't have to ask twice." He adjusted the mainsheet.

The boat kicked up some spray. María wiped the salt from her brow and cried out. "This is bliss, Father!"

Immediately, Pedro's heart dropped to his toes. By

reminding him of his clerical collar, she'd transported him back to the world of Iglesia del Espíritu Santo—a place he was determined to escape from, at least for today.

"Please." He almost felt he was begging. "Out here, at least, call me Pedro. You don't know me very well yet, but I'm no longer so enamored with the priesthood. Somehow it's important to me that you know that."

María lost the smile on her face momentarily, until a wave slammed into the bow, sending an arc of spray over them both. She adjusted her grip and held the wheel steady.

"Well, Pedro's fine with me! I'm not exactly a big fan of Mother Church. She and I parted ways a long time ago."

They continued on without saying more. As far as Pedro was concerned, they could stay on this course forever.

As they munched on the sandwiches he'd brought along, Pedro tried to explain his love of sailing. "Constant adjustment is the rule of the sea and the sail. I like that and I'm good at it. But on land, keeping my life heading where I want isn't so easy."

María acknowledged his soliloquy with a sad nod of her head.

"And these days," Pedro continued, "I'm beginning to realize that the course I took years ago to become a priest wasn't really the course for which I'm suited."

"Yes, I understand," she replied after a few moments of silence. "We make decisions about our lives, and then the world turns out different from how we imagined. We all face the need to change, even if we don't want to."

Pedro listened carefully, noting with relief that his idea of having mistakenly become a priest didn't upset her. "I haven't spoken this easily with a woman since college," Pedro said wistfully, remembering Isabel. "It's comfortable talking with you."

María's face reddened. She blushed easily, thought Pedro. Have I embarrassed her, or is it the wine we had with lunch?

"Anytime you want, Pedro, I'm glad to listen."

Silence fell again as they both contemplated what they had just said.

"It is a very peaceful feeling out here." María broke the silence. "It makes me joyful, like playing the piano. Like how you feel when the power of a minor seventh resolves into a major chord."

"I saw your piano and I wondered if you played. Perhaps you will play for me sometime?"

"Aye, aye, captain."

As they neared the coast, a gray Cuban patrol boat approached and circled at a distance of sixty yards. The dark barrels of its deck guns seemed as menacing as the spines of a sea urchin. Pedro could see binoculars examining them. The patrol boat circled twice and then sped away, sending up a huge wake. *La Rosa Blanca* tossed about violently, its owner grinding his teeth — in fury or fear, Pedro wasn't sure.

Chapter 11

Concentrating on his Sunday homily while basking in the remembrance of the sail with María, Pedro started when his phone rang, killing the tranquility. It was Dolores insisting on an immediate meeting of the Defarge Circle.

"But I'm having trouble with my sermon. As usual, I'm not sure what to say. Can't this wait until—"

"Father, there's no time. I need you now!" Her tone was emphatic, on the verge of explosive. Perhaps if he consented to a short meeting, he would return to his desk with some fresh ideas.

"Where do you want to get together? Here?" he asked.

"No. Let's meet five doors down the street from Las Palmas Café. Remember it? The café owner lives there, and he's a friend." Pedro thought back to that wonderful afternoon when he and María had killed time in the café's garden while the drugs were spirited away from his parked car.

"Be sure you're not followed," Dolores added.

"You're always imagining enemies."

Pedro shook his head. Batista's security police were powerful, but they couldn't be everywhere.

"It's what keeps me alive. It would serve you well to do the same. And on the way, stop in front of María's office. She'll come out—I'll tell her three forty-five. Don't be late!"

"But it's Saturday—why is she at her office today?"

"Some shakeup or something," Dolores was sounding impatient. "I don't know, and I don't care. Be there on time!"

María. Just hearing her name made Pedro sigh. He put on his cassock and collar and hurried to his Plymouth. As he drove off, he found himself watching the rearview mirror for anyone who might be following. There was no tail that he could see, but Dolores's caution had had its effect. He made a beeline to El Tribunal de Cuentas and María. Beautiful María.

Pedro, María, and six other members of the Defarge Circle made it to the modest home of the owner of Las Palmas Café well before four o'clock. Dolores arrived characteristically late. The others were seated when she came in, with María sitting next to Pedro on a loveseat. Dolores was dressed conservatively in a knee-length skirt and sweater. She sat down without a smile or an apology for her tardiness. Clearly, something important had happened, and she wasted no time telling them what it was.

"There's an attack going on at Alto Songo," she said in a voice just above a whisper. "That's an army barracks in Oriente Province. We're going to take it together with hundreds of prisoners. This revolution is coming to an end very shortly."

"That sounds like a major undertaking for Fidel," said Pedro. "But I've been reading about the army rounding up rebels in the plains and also in the Sierra Maestra. Things don't seem to be going as well as you say."

"Don't believe *anything* you read in the press," said Dolores. "Batista controls every word. Look what happened in fifty-six: all the papers said Fidel was killed when he came over from Mexico in the *Granma*. Even when the *New York Times* reporter Matthews published his stories about meeting Fidel in the mountains, Batista insisted that he'd been bribed to say that. It wasn't until the *Times* published the pictures of Matthews smoking a cigar with Fidel that Batista finally admitted that maybe he'd been wrong about Fidel's death."

"That is exciting news," said María. "The sooner we can speak without fear and have a free press, the better for all of us."

"Yes, we'll finally have a democracy," said Dolores. "But we still have more battles to fight before it's all over. We're going to take a lot of casualties at Alto Songo. And we're using up armaments. That's why I need help."

"What do you need? More penicillin?" Pedro didn't look forward to another trip to his father's office to obtain medicine. Since Alberto's death, Dr. Villanueva spent most of his days looking out his window. He had cancelled 90 percent of his appointments.

"Guns and ammunition," said Dolores.

"Armaments are a bit outside our line of work!" Juan Gómez, the polo player/engineer, protested. "Where do you think we're going to get them?"

The members grumbled to each other, clearly not happy with Dolores's pronouncement.

"No, no, you misunderstand," said Dolores. "I don't want you to *supply* the guns—I want some of you to help *transport* them. We smuggled in a shipment of Bren light machine guns that are the latest technology. They're a big improvement over the war surplus we've been using."

Dolores looked directly at Pedro.

"This is where you come in."

"Me?" asked Pedro. "How can *I* help? Moreover, why *should* I help?"

Pedro frantically searched for words to dodge this assignment. "When I joined up, I told you that I'd help with anything but guns, and I've done that. God, have I ever done that." He looked around the room to the other members of the Circle, then back at Dolores.

She stared at him, a withering look on her face.

"There must be others who can drive whatever you need up there," he pleaded, his hands clasped together as if in church.

"Father, don't forget yourself here. We're in an army, and I am your *comandante*. I'm not asking for permission."

"But Pasionaria," María spoke up, "that's never been the way we operate in the Circle."

"You people don't realize—we're on the cusp of a new era. If we push hard now, the regime will topple. The Defarge Circle isn't a knitting club, it's a quartermaster platoon, and it's got to do its part in this last push of the revolution. Democracy is within our grasp!"

"Yes, but why must it be me?" asked Pedro. "I've already lost a brother, I've rescued your driver, and I've delivered the antibiotics. My father barely speaks to me."

"I told you when you volunteered to provide the antibiotics that my interest in you was your sailing skills."

"What's sailing got to do with this?" Pedro asked.

"Listen, Father." Dolores honeyed her tone. "If we could drive to the mountains, we have many people who could help. But Batista has all the roads blocked between here and the Sierra Maestra. There's fighting everywhere in the central plains, impossible to get a truck through. There are roadblocks everywhere. The guns are already here in Havana Harbor, and we have to get them up to Fidel! That's where you come in. You just have to take a few days' sail over to the east end of the island. No sweat and the guns can get to where they can do the most good."

"You don't understand," Pedro protested. "I'm not afraid for myself. But my parents have already lost one son. When I got you the penicillin, I promised my father that I wouldn't take further risks for the cause. And now you want me to break my promise to my father."

"If it weren't a crisis, I wouldn't ask. I don't want you to break any promises to your father, but I want you to keep your promise to your country! I know about your brother—Alberto, that was his name, no? He gave his life to save someone who was a prisoner in La Cabaña. Think of how many lives we will save from La Cabaña once Batista is toppled!"

Pedro didn't know how to respond. He felt torn between not wanting to cause his parents more pain and finishing what he'd started with Alberto. Alberto—the very mention of his name made Pedro sick to his stomach. The image of his brother's flag-draped body flashed in his mind's eye. His mother's terrible keening at the loss of her son echoed in his brain. Alberto had died saving *one* person from La Cabaña. Could he save countless more by bringing Batista down?

"Why me?" he asked. "What makes you think I can get past the patrol boats?"

"Your boat is a common sight in the waters off Havana. Even if you're observed, you won't attract much attention. And once you get east of Havana, it's a large ocean."

"When do you need this done?" Pedro asked.

"Yesterday," said Dolores.

"I'll have to make arrangements for a replacement during my absence from Espíritu Santo. I can't just leave without a word." Pedro's mind raced.

"I'll say that the death of my brother has deeply saddened me, and that I need to take some time off."

Pedro knew his logic was believable; he did need a

rest. And he couldn't help noticing the approving faces of the group, Dolores and María especially.

He hastened on. "And I'll tell my parents the same."

Dolores gave Pedro instructions about their meeting place two days hence, as well as enlisting other men in the group to ready the guns for shipment.

As she talked on like the quartermaster she was, Pedro whispered to María, "When the meeting's over, I'd like to drive you home."

Pedro's aside came out louder than he'd intended. No sooner had he spoken than Dolores shot him a disapproving frown.

Later, heading for La Víbora, the couple watched the sky darken. In the distance, flashes of lightning outlined storm clouds that swept in from the sea.

Although it was only late afternoon, Pedro switched on his headlights. "The radio said there would be a storm. Are you worried?"

"No, I'm worried about you," María replied. She did seem concerned; she was trembling.

"You haven't been in our group very long, and it seems to me that you've been carrying more than your weight."

"But Pasionaria has a point—this is a war, and if we have a chance to end it, shouldn't that be the most important thing?"

"Yes, but why must it be *you?*"

It started to rain, and Pedro switched on the windshield wipers. "I'm thinking of how happy my parishioners were to get their kid out of La Cabaña. Think how many others could be saved if the revolution came to a quick end."

"You just don't get it!" María cried out. "Pull this car over—now!" The Plymouth swerved across the slick pavement and skidded to a stop next to a park. There wasn't a soul in sight.

"I feel like I'm missing something," Pedro said.

María wiped her nose with her handkerchief.

"What's wrong?" Pedro touched her shoulder. "Pasionaria's probably right. No one will notice me out there. You saw it yourself—the navy boat was just yards away, and they turned and sailed off without so much as an adios."

"I don't want you to go," María said slowly, turning toward him. "I know you can feel what's between us."

Pedro was stunned. Thanks be to God, this exceptional woman shared his emotions. He took her hand and kissed it.

"You don't know how long I've wanted to do that," he said gravely, reaching up and removing his collar. She inched closer to him and gently kissed first his cheek and then his lips.

Pedro returned her kiss, gently at first, until his desire awakened. María's lips parted, and their kiss became more electric; their tongues intertwined—touching, tasting. A low groan from Pedro. He ran his fingers through María's hair as he slowly pulled away from her. Was this all real? If I let her go, he thought, will she disappear?

"What do we do now?" asked María, breaking the silence that followed.

Pedro, feeling her warm breath on his neck, knew he had no compass to navigate this course. "We do what we must," he said, not at all sure what he meant.

She sat upright and straightened her hair. "I guess to start with, I must get home. I promised the kids I'd take them to the Tencen for an early supper. Their favorite is the special burger with the chopped ham, mayonnaise, and pickle relish."

Pedro shifted into reality drive. "Yes, Father Domingo says that Woolworth's has the best lunch counter in Havana."

Pedro drove away from the park in pouring rain, confused but happy. Closer to home, the storm intensified. When they pulled up to the house, María said, "Maybe it's not such a good idea to take the kids out."

Pedro was disappointed. "Don't worry, they'll be fine. I just don't want this evening to end quite yet."

María smiled. "Neither do I."

"I didn't want to be Pasionaria's errand boy before this, and now I really don't want to sail off and leave you," Pedro said. He was thinking that there might be a storm outside the car, but inside there was only a bright, sunny day. He embraced again the saltiness of her lips, and the warmth of her breasts. Those memories would comfort him no matter what lay ahead.

Chapter 12

But the next two days brought Pedro back to reality. He got nothing substantial done. Instead, he paced the floor of his sitting room and fretted. He, Father Pedro Villanueva, a priest, a padre, committed to a life of chastity, had fallen in love with a woman who could be one of his parishioners. To add to the deception, he was now torn between being with María always and doing his duty as a member of the revolution. He packed and repacked his duffel bag four times. He took his time in finding a substitute at the church for a few weeks. He stuttered when he informed his parents and Domingo that he needed a rest and was going to visit a classmate in Guantánamo. When they all appeared to believe fully that a good sail would provide a much-needed change, he reflected how easy deception had become a part of his life. One step at a time, he told himself.

Luckily, *La Rosa Blanca* sailed north without attracting attention from the government boat that patrolled the mouth of the bay. He turned east when he was six miles off the coast and in international waters, running wing on wing parallel to the coast. The horizon was clear of any other boats.

As the sun set behind him, he made his way south to the harbor at Cojimar, the small fishing village where he was to take on his cargo. Darkness was coming quickly. Close to the cove near the village, he spotted a red light high on a turret of an old fort, a prearranged signal. He scrambled for his flashlight, pointed at the shoreline, and slid the switch. Nothing. Damn! He'd been instructed to signal back. Desperate, he unscrewed the top of the metal cap and inspected the battery contact. In the fading dusk, he reached into his pocket and drew out a jackknife. Feeling his way like a blind man, he opened the blade and used it to scratch at the battery contacts. He screwed back the lid and slid the switch. Again, nothing. He gave the flashlight a smack against the side of the boat again, and the darkness filled with bright white light, causing Pedro to almost drop the flashlight overboard. What a jerk I am, he thought, an unqualified jerk. I can't do anything remotely practical. As he quickly shut the light off, two flashes came back from across the harbor.

He pointed *La Rosa Blanca* in the direction of the flashes. In less than fifteen minutes, Pedro had made it across the bay and turned the sloop into the wind. As he anchored about thirty yards offshore, he could hear music in the distance. How far the source was, he wasn't sure; he'd learned that sound travels a long way over water.

The sun had vanished past the horizon, and the line

106

between sea and sky blurred, becoming a continuous dark indigo. Pedro could make out a few beached fishing boats; their nets hung from poles like giant spiderwebs. A few campfires burned along the beach. From the shore, a muffled creak drew his attention until he could just barely discern a skiff moving toward him, faintly visible against the darkened shoreline. When it neared him, he saw a solitary figure in the bow; it was Dolores.

"*Hola,* Padre," Dolores whispered. "You're right on schedule. When we take over, we're going to have to put you in charge of the trains."

The boat came alongside Pedro, and two brawny men picked up burlap sacks like field hands hefting potatoes. They passed the bundles up to Pedro, until the small skiff was empty. Then, with Pedro helping, they carried the cargo down the companionway to the galley and to the forward cabin. After everything was stowed, the two men helped Dolores aboard.

"Okay, Father, let's shove off."

When he looked dubious, she added, "I want to make sure you don't have any trouble on the other end."

"Have you ever sailed before?" Pedro asked.

"Of course! Don't you remember where we met? We do more than dance at the Havana Yacht Club, don't we, Father?"

"But there's only food and water for one in the galley."

"I've got that all taken care of," Dolores said, patting a backpack over her shoulders.

Pedro was unhappy about the change of plan. He would have preferred to make his mistakes and consult his guilt in private. It did make some sense for Dolores to come along, though. After all, she knew the rebels on the other end and Pedro did not. What if he got to the destination and handed the guns and ammunition over to the wrong person? There was little sense arguing with her, anyway. She might be gorgeous, but she was a take-no-prisoners female. Plus, she knew the territory. And she could spell him at the wheel, allowing him to get some rest along the way. The trip would be faster with her along.

"What's our destination? It might be useful to know."

"Just head east toward Baracoa. I'll tell you exactly where we're going when we get closer."

"Right you are," Pedro said. "Take your gear below and then come back on deck. There's work to be done."

"What are your orders, my captain?" she asked a few minutes later, throwing him a mock salute.

Pedro pointed to the bow. "Go forward and raise the anchor. I'll raise the mainsail."

Within five minutes, *La Rosa Blanca* slipped quietly from her anchorage. The waves rolled gently by as they sailed east, and Pedro kept her at least six miles offshore to minimize the chance of running into the coast guard. With a cabin full of machine guns and ammunition, it wasn't the time to have a shipboard consultation with Batista's friends.

Despite his familiarity with *La Rosa Blanca*, feeling her respond in the darkness was eerie and unsettling. With not enough moonlight to see much ahead, and no illumination for the compass, Pedro had difficulty checking course headings. Without being able to see beyond the bow, he found that the boat rolled through troughs of waves that seemed to come out of nowhere. Fortunately, the wind was light but steady; it would take a lot to capsize her. He wondered if Dolores ever got seasick.

They made good speed despite the light winds due to the Gulf Stream current. And Dolores behaved as if she'd been at sea all her life and was a regular mate on *La Rosa Blanca*. After reaching international waters, Dolores went down to the galley. In less than a half hour, she returned with two plates of grilled Cuban sandwiches nestled next to fried plantains. A beer bottle stuck out from each of her fatigue jacket pockets. Pedro was impressed.

"You're a woman of many talents. I see you figured out the alcohol stove. The sandwich is perfectly toasted."

"No problems below, captain. I hope you enjoy it, but don't tell Luis that I can cook. I'm not going to be the little woman in this show."

Dolores took a seat close to Pedro.

"Luis? Is he going to be there?"

"Yes, that's the plan. He can't wait to get his hands on these guns."

Pedro replied with his mouth full.

"I'm sure that he's just as interested in reuniting with you. He must miss you. A man gets lonely, too." Pedro popped the cap from his bottle of beer and washed down the tasty pork.

"I'm sure he needs the company of his most attractive comrade-in-arms," Pedro chattered on.

"You think me attractive? I thought priests didn't notice that sort of thing."

Pedro threw caution to the winds.

"I'm about as poor an example of a priest right now as you could find. For a long time I've been thinking I'm not suited for the Church. Part of the problem is just what you're asking—I'm a priest, but I'm still a man."

He knew he was saying too much, confiding his weakness to Dolores. He should send her to bed, let her get some sleep to spell him later.

"You said that being a man is only part of the problem—what's the other part?" Dolores seemed extremely interested in his confessions.

"I became a priest because I thought I could help people. Over the years, I've been finding that there's little I do—baptisms, marriages, funerals. We've got major problems with the poor and the sick that the Church needs to deal with, and the archdiocese turns a blind eye. The government is corrupt and the Church is silent. No one can visit La Cabaña and not want to scream at the top of his lungs. And the Church—again silent!" Pedro's voice cried out to the dark night.

Dolores took a long swig from her beer and wiped her lips with her hand.

"All I can say is that I picked the right priest to take on. The revolution needs you, but it seems that you need the revolution even more!"

"You may be right. I knew Fidel in school. He was the best athlete at Belén. All the boys wanted to be like him. And he was smart. Even the teachers seemed intimidated. If anyone can unseat Batista, it's Fidel."

"He's certainly got luck on his side. It's enough to make *me* believe in miracles. The revolution needs a little miracle here or there. Right now, I'm going to hit the sack. Fidel can wait until I get some sleep."

Pedro watched as Dolores opened the hatch to the companionway and descended the ladder. Her voluptuous curves, silhouetted by the cabin lights, disappeared below.

At dawn, Dolores popped her head up through the companionway, wearing clamdiggers and a yellow shirt. "Time for me to take over."

"I think I want to watch you handle her for a while, before I knock off," Pedro said. "I just want to make sure you can keep us on course and right side up, if I'm going to get any sleep."

She took the helm and appeared quite comfortable.

"What's our heading?" she asked.

"I've been trying to keep us on a ninety-degree

course. Soon, we should head south. For now, keep on the same heading, and we'll turn south after I get some sleep."

"Yes, captain." Dolores gave him another mock salute. Pedro watched her handle the wheel and adjust the trim of the jib. She clearly knew what she was doing.

"Where did you learn to sail?" Pedro asked.

"Cal Poly. Couldn't spend all my time with those engineers and their slide rules. They think they're stylishly dressed if both their socks are the same color."

Pedro laughed. She could be amusing and enjoyable when she wanted to be.

"I've never sailed in the Pacific," he said. "From what I've read, the waves can be pretty treacherous over there."

"Never had much of a problem," said Dolores.

"Hope things stay calm like this," Pedro said, removing his eyes from Dolores's legs and over the bow at the gentle roll of the waves. "I think we'll be lucky today."

"Feel lucky, Padre. We've got enough guns and ammo down there to land us both in La Cabaña for a very long time, if not in front of the wall!"

Pedro felt his stomach lurch. He smelled again the stench of death that had pervaded La Cabaña. Rembering the untimely death of Alberto reminded him that he wasn't on a pleasure cruise.

"You seem to have everything under control," Pedro said. His head was spinning, either from fatigue or nervousness, he couldn't tell. "I think I'll go below."

On the bunk that Dolores had left unmade, he fell asleep wrapped in her sheet, still scented vaguely of cinnamon. He dreamed of travel. He was taking a plane somewhere and felt the vibration of the plane's engine as it taxied down the tarmac. The plane came to a stop. The motors roared, and he woke up. He was still in the berth of *La Rosa Blanca*, but he could hear the plane's engines. He climbed up the ladder, squinting in the bright sun of the afternoon. Dolores was at the wheel staring into the sky. A plane, not two hundred feet above the boat, buzzed past, as Dolores waved and gave the plane's pilot a big smile.

"I'm glad you're up, Padre. We have a visitor. Quick, sit next to me and put your arm around me," she commanded.

Pedro stepped behind the wheel and slung his arm around her shoulder. She turned to him and kissed him on the mouth.

"We have to give him something to remember," she said.

Dazed, Pedro fixed his gaze on her.

"Look up and wave to the nice pilot," she said.

Pedro glanced up; the Cuban Air Force plane was making another run at them. He and Dolores both waved. The plane rocked from side to side in greeting. Slowly, it disappeared over the horizon.

"I think we better sail south and check our position," Pedro said shakily.

Dolores disentangled herself from Pedro's arms, moved to the center of the cockpit and, in the slow motion of a striptease, removed her pants and shirt. When she shimmied naked back to him, he held his breath. Her body was lean and taut, her breasts small, perfect. His penis stiffened. When she joined him again at the wheel, Pedro instinctively brought the bow into the wind, stopping the boat in seconds.

She laughed wickedly. "Let's really give oglers something to look at."

She pulled him away from the wheel and pressed herself against him, all toughness and cinnamon. Without thought, Pedro's hands began to explore her body as they kissed.

Dolores sank to the floor of the cockpit, pulling Pedro on top of her. He couldn't move, nor did he want to. She grasped his shorts and adeptly, almost without notice, slipped them down his legs.

She purred. "I admit, I like a challenge, and you're that, for sure. I've stayed awake some nights wondering what you'd feel like against my skin. Have *you?*"

Without a thought of any consequences other than pleasure, Pedro tipped Dolores's head back and clamped his mouth down on hers. His longtime chastity disappeared like a puff of smoke, the devil's puff of smoke. His kiss was primal, erupting from pent-up lust and need. Dolores stroked him gently. Pedro hissed sharply at her touch.

"Are you as ready as I am?" Dolores whispered. "Can you do it?"

Her challenge drove him mad. His hands went wild over her body. "Now!" she commanded, and instantly he was inside her. The sail luffed noisily overhead as her hips rose up to meet his every thrust, spiraling Pedro into an altered state of consciousness. His blood pounded in his ears; he felt like he was drowning. Only when he heard Dolores moan with pleasure did he find his release. He buried his face in her dark-brown hair, afraid to look at her, to see on her face satisfaction at gaining control. You fool, he thought, in a postcoital spasm of guilt, the world's spinning way beyond you.

"Mmm, my sweet María—"

"What?!" Dolores pushed him off her. "What the hell did you just say?"

"Your name," he stammered.

"Grow up!" she taunted.

Embarrassed, he took back the wheel and tried to look nonchalant as he searched for his shorts.

"What will Luis think?"

Dolores incinerated him with that Carmen-like look of contempt he had once admired.

"Are you planning on telling him, Padre?"

She gathered up her clothes and disappeared down the companionway.

The voyage lasted two and a half days through reasonably calm seas, with swells never exceeding three feet, but whitecaps as far as the eye could see. Only once, while Dolores slept during Pedro's watch, was there a squall. The storm passed in less than an hour. Pedro felt it was nothing to compare with the squall in his mind. He hadn't touched Dolores once since they'd made love. She, on the other hand, appeared to have completely forgotten the incident. And *she'd* been worried about going to hell!

Sometimes Pedro stared at the dots of light on ships twinkling in the distance that seemed to vanish only to reappear seconds later, always on the same course. He held to his own course and prayed. He had worse problems than wayward ships.

Full of doubt that anyone was interested in his prayers, he tortured himself. I've now changed from a mere venial sinner to a mortal sinner. What kind of man have I become? It's one thing to abandon the priesthood and break my mother's heart, but to fall in love with one woman and lust after another—is there nothing I won't do? Have I lost my rudder completely?

Once more he contrasted the sea and his spiritual life ashore. At sea, we have rules—red, right returning for lights—upwind sloops have right-of-way—what are my rules for myself as a priest and as a man? He had no answers.

Chapter 13

Dolores came up from the galley the next morning with a mug of coffee for Pedro, who'd been at the wheel all night. She was dressed in green fatigues. "Do you know where we are?" she asked.

Pedro noted that she was now wasting no time on chitchat. He pointed to his navigation charts. "I've just been looking at these. See that notch in the stone wall of that mountain? That's Sierra Cristal. When I was a boy, my family used to swim off the beach of Cayo Nipe Grande over there."

Dolores stared into the distance. "You've made good progress, Padre. It won't be much longer."

"Longer to where? You've never really told me what our destination is, other than sail east toward Baracoa.

Dolores spread out the chart. "Let me see, we're here—so, see this little town over here? That's Moa."

Pedro strained to look. keeping one hand on the wheel.

"This past June, Raúl Castro captured the town with Luis's help and took a bunch of American hostages. Fidel wasn't too happy about the hostage taking, I'm afraid, but we wanted to show the world that the revolution was gaining steam. Raúl let the prisoners go, and they couldn't say enough good things about how nicely they were treated. It was a huge P.R. stunt!"

"And we're going there?" Pedro asked.

"That's the idea," Dolores answered.

Pedro checked his charts. "There's a break in the reef at Cayo Moa Grande. What do we do once we get into the bay?"

Dolores crouched on the cockpit floor and hunched over the map. "Well, Luis controls Moa, but there's still danger from the air, so we're going to sail northwest past this point that looks like a finger," said Dolores, indicating a peninsula. Then we'll head up the coast about a mile."

She stabbed at the chart. "There are a few houses over here, and we can anchor in the cove near them. That's where we'll meet Luis."

"Rough and dirty," replied Pedro. "But we've only got sixty miles to go."

Pedro was at the helm when *La Rosa Blanca* slipped into the cove. Spotting a campfire on the beach. Pedro made the sign of the cross without thinking, then pointed his flashlight toward the fire and signaled twice.

In a few minutes, a skiff made its way alongside. In the moonlight, Pedro saw a militiaman with a scraggy mustache reaching out to hold the side of the sloop.

"Luis! Luis, darling!" Dolores shouted, her white teeth aglow in the light of the skiff's lantern. One of Luis's men fastened a towline to the bow of *La Rosa Blanca* and towed the sloop through a narrow channel into a protected cove.

When they all made it ashore, Dolores threw her arms around Luis's neck, kissing him with fervor. Luis staggered to keep his balance. "I see you've brought a guest," he grunted.

"*Comandante*, may I present Father Pedro Villanueva," Dolores said.

Luis bowed deeply, like a maître d', spreading out his arms in an exaggerated greeting. He wore a bandolier strung across his chest and rosary beads wrapped around his military cap sitting atop curly black hair.

"Welcome, my friend, to our little resort," he said, "We've been waiting since last night. I welcome you to the revolution." Luis held out his hand.

"The Father was the one who got medical help to save poor Jorge back in Havana," Dolores said.

Upon hearing this news, Luis bypassed Pedro's extended right hand and hugged him like a lost brother.

The area next to the cove was thickly wooded. Luis's men removed the precious cargo from *La Rosa Blanca*, then covered her deck with palm fronds. With her sails down and stowed, and her mast parallel to the vertical lines of the trees, she was invisible to reconnaissance flights and anyone searching from offshore, safe for the time being.

In a clearing under the protection of the tree canopy, the rebels could move around the encampment without being spotted from the air. Pedro, Dolores, and Luis joined the guerillas around the campfire. Looking at Luis in the firelight, Pedro observed that he was built as solid as a tank, but not quite as tall as the towering tree that he knew Fidel to be. Unlike the other rebels, whose bushy beards and unshorn hair gave them a ferocious aura, Luis was clean shaven, except for a pencil mustache. Luis made sure that Pedro was given food and a metal cup of rum, then he and Dolores disappeared into the forest amidst laughter and hooting from the other rebels. My sailing companion is totally amoral, Pedro thought sadly.

After he'd finished the grilled chicken he'd been given, Pedro was led to a lean-to made of felled palm trunks covered by fronds, handed a blanket, and wished a goodnight by a young "guerrilla" who reminded Pedro of Roberto, María's oldest child. Pedro knew from Dolores and María that the revolution wasn't just an enterprise for men; women were an integral part of bringing change to Cuba, but to understand that adolescents were part of the rebel forces was sobering.

Pedro slept restlessly. When he awoke, the band of guerrillas was already packing up. Next to him on the ground was a knapsack, a set of olive-green fatigues, and a pair of boots. After he packed his sailing clothes in the knapsack, he found Dolores and Luis sitting together on a large boulder drinking coffee. Dolores was in her fatigues, sporting a black beret. It was hard to believe that she was the naked, ardent woman he'd made love to on the deck of his boat. He scowled in her direction.

I wonder what she sees in Luis, thought Pedro, as he examined the rebel commander. She's an amazing woman. He glanced at the carbine she held on her lap. I bet she knows how to use that gun, too. I wouldn't want to test her.

"Good morning, Father," said Dolores sweetly and, Pedro thought, dismissively. "Sleep well?"

Luis grunted a greeting. He didn't appear to be a morning person.

"Not too bad," Pedro replied.

"We need to get away from the coast and into the mountains," Dolores advised.

"I thought I was going back to Havana."

Pedro waited for Dolores to protest, but instead it was Luis Ferrer who asked, "You mean you want to leave us, comrade? I don't think that's such a good idea."

"Why? I've delivered your guns. What's left for me to do now?"

Luis frowned as if he were not used to being questioned. "Our men haven't seen a priest for months. I think you should come with us and listen to confession and whatever else you priests do for people."

"Be nice, Luis," said Dolores. "The Father is our guest."

"Well, our guest knows our position and about the new guns. If he sails away now and is captured, we'll all be in deep shit. It's healthier if he stays with us."

"You see," said Dolores looking at Pedro with a resigned smile, "there's no choice—that's the nature of revolution and war. You have to learn to adapt—and not whine."

There was no sense in arguing.

Dolores handed him a black leather belt from which hung a revolver. "Take this, Father. You never know."

"I don't know anything about firearms. I'm a priest," protested Pedro, eyeing the gunmetal.

"Suit yourself," Dolores said. "We're going on a difficult hike through some tough passes and steep climbs. It's fairly primitive. Who knows what we'll meet?"

"Okay," Pedro said reluctantly, and strapped on the gun. His worries of the night before were already starting to be fulfilled. He thought he had escaped being a priest in Batista's Havana, only to return to being a priest again, but this time a priest with a firearm.

Chapter 14

Pedro knew little about the Sierra Maestra range. Once, as a schoolboy, he had camped out for three days somewhere in the mountains. All he remembered about the experience was being stung by a bee. Now, as the guerrilla group trekked across a plain full of more varieties of palm trees than he knew existed, he was glad that he was wearing sturdy boots. But over the next two days, as the small band climbed up into small hills, larger hills, and into the mountainous region of Pico Turquino, he realized he was terribly out of shape. He breathed heavily and straggled behind the rest, as they climbed higher and higher, and then descended through more paths that had been hacked out of the rugged terrain.

Occasionally, the group stopped to rest. The meager rations consisted mostly of maize and sweet potatoes, which explained why the guerrillas, with the exception of Luis, were emaciated. Somehow, they found the strength to drag themselves, hungry as they were, up and down the mountain trails, each weighed down with a rifle and backpack. No doubt their strength lay in their devotion to the cause. Fortunately, tiny, agile mules that were heavily loaded with supplies scampered ahead, as if carrying the weapons and ammunition was a day in the park.

The trails were bordered by undergrowth—thick stands of ferns the size of a man, bushes with menacing thorns. Coffee trees and cedars grew unchecked, and dense ceiba forests, whose canopies blocked the sun for much of the trip, also protected them from detection by Batista's air force. Occasionally, Pedro heard the sound of an aircraft overhead, but the guerrillas never slackened their pace. An explosion of parrot cries and yellow wings once startled the forward column. Pedro welcomed the color and variety. He had never seen wild parrots before.

During a rest stop, Pedro observed Luis carefully. Seated on a fallen tree, smoking a pipe, he looked more like a history professor than a revolutionary, which was ironic. From his rough speech, Pedro knew that Luis had never been an academic and was a stranger to the halls of schools such as Belén. Not a scholar like Fidel.

Pedro tried to draw him into a conversation, but Luis seemed more interested in pontification.

"Just wait, Father, when our glorious July twenty-six movement takes over, those capitalists are going to piss their pants!" Luis boasted.

Dizzy from the climb in the heat, his legs aching, his hamstrings protesting, Pedro thought, for the love of God, do we have to engage in dialectic now?

"I'm sure there will be many positive changes," Pedro agreed neutrally. "The government is corrupt. Nothing gets done unless you're a friend of the president. Protestors are jailed without cause. I know. I've seen it myself. And my brother was murdered—"

"It's all going to be different," Luis interrupted. "The streets will run red with the changes we're going to bring."

"I hope not," Pedro replied. "I've seen quite enough death in the streets and prisons of Havana." He could still smell the deaths he'd witnessed.

"Sometimes you need to shed a little blood to heal the diseases that those gringo devils have brought to our beautiful island," said Luis. "Without U.S. support, Batista would have been history years ago. Those imperialists control all the mines and the sugar. They've raped our country since we broke loose from Spain, and it's time for payback. Even your precious church will have to answer."

"Luis," Dolores cautioned, "he's here to help us."

Luis took a long drag on his pipe. He raised his head and formed a perfect circle with his lips. Blowing upward, he created a big, round plume of smoke that first formed above his head like a sooty halo, then wafted higher until it vanished.

"A helpful priest? Now I've seen everything." Luis said.

Pedro considered. He's right—too long we've lived in the shadow of the United States, but there's a darkness to Luis that I don't remember in Fidel. Pedro watched as Luis pulled Dolores onto his lap and buried his face in her chest.

"You're good enough to eat," he mumbled.

Pedro gaped. Ferrer was really in love with Dolores and didn't care who knew it. And any scruples she might have about her encounter with Pedro had been definitively put aside. Pedro kicked the gound in disgust, recalling the smoothness of her skin and her erotic touch. I'm a wicked deceiver, but so is she. And only one of us has a conscience.

Finally, the band arrived at a clearing. Here, under another ceiba canopy, dozens of armed men and women were readying themselves for battle. A blacksmith pounded on an anvil, fashioning harnesses for the mules. At a makeshift table, three guerrillas poured gunpowder into small metal containers. Others distributed ammunition and weapons. An unpainted building with a red cross on the door, and constructed of scraps of wood haphazardly nailed together, served as the hospital. To Pedro, all this preparation signaled danger.

"You'll sleep in here," Luis said. "This is the encampment where we meet visitors. Fidel's not likely to make a special appearance for a priest, though. Remember what Marx said about religion."

"Luis!" Dolores said. "Be respectful!"

"Yes, yes. You're right, as always." Luis turned toward Pedro. "I'm sorry if I offended you. I appreciate your balls. I'm sure Fidel will want to meet you."

To Dolores, he asked, "Now, was that nice enough?"

• • •

It felt good to sleep, even with sheets that weren't clean and with mosquitoes as big as airplanes. The next morning after breakfast, Dolores gave Pedro the orders of the day.

"We're going to mount an offensive. I want you to meet with some of the devout Catholic boys who are an important part of our forces."

In a few minutes, a young soldier, about fifteen, approached and introduced himself as Fernando Damaso. Fernando had dark skin, and teeth that no dentist had ever examined.

"Sit down, my son," Pedro said. "Where are you from?"

"Santiago."

Pedro inspected the skinny boy and wondered why he wasn't in school. "How long have you been up here?"

"Not long, only a few weeks."

"How long since you had confession?"

"Too long."

"Do you want to confess?" Not for the first time, Pedro hated the mechanical process.

"Yes. Bless me, Father, for I have sinned."

"How have you sinned?" Pedro asked.

The boy fidgeted, then said, "I'm frightened, Father."

"It is not a sin to be afraid."

"Yes, but I don't know if I'm strong enough to pull a trigger. I know that's what I'm supposed to do. I want to win the revolution, but I've never even killed a chicken. I'm a city boy."

"It's not a sin to kill in the defense of freedom," said Pedro. "An evil man is strangling our country. We are helping do God's work."

Pedro thought of the revolver he was carrying. He was as innocent of killing machines as the boy. From signing on to deliver guns, he was now carrying one and expected to use it.

He crossed himself and blessed the boy. "Be careful and may God protect you. And, if you would, please show me how my gun works." Trying to raise the boy's spirits, he joked. "There are no operating instructions."

The boy gave Pedro a wide smile that revealed the extent of his rotten teeth. Very seriously, Fernando took the revolver from Pedro and checked to see if it was loaded. He opened the cylinder and pointed the gun upward, allowing the cartridges to fall into his palm. Then he pointed the gun to the ground and pulled the trigger. The hammer went snap, but there was no explosion.

"Just checking," Fernando said, and demonstrated all the features of the gun including releasing the safety, taking aim at an imaginary target, and gently squeezing the trigger. Then he showed Pedro how to reload the cylinder. In the middle of what Pedro considered to be a very interesting tutoring, the drone of a low-flying airplane engine could be heard, and the rebels in the encampment scattered to douse any open fires. The plane took a second run past the camp and then flew out of sight.

Dolores announced. "Father, we've got to split! That plane means trouble. There's a column of regular army coming our way. It won't be long before this place is crawling with soldiers."

She introduced him to Colonel Enrique León. The colonel, standing ramrod straight, was considerably taller than Luis and had thick black hair with a pronounced widows peak.

"Stay with him," she commanded, then ran off to help Luis direct the exodus from the encampment.

Pedro and Fernando stared at each other. Now they were comrades. Neither had a choice. They couldn't run away or hide behind a tree; they were part of the band.

Quickly, he and the boy followed Colonel León.

"Take your time, Father," instructed the colonel. "We can let a little space open up between us and the rear of the column."

Pedro choked down the bile in his throat. He was heading to the front line of the revolution armed only with his crucifix and a five-minute lesson on how to shoot. The rest of the men, as calm as if they were in church, strapped on their revolvers, shouldered their rifles, and lashed bandoliers of grenades to their chests. Some carried the new machine guns over their shoulders.

Pedro swatted at a swarm of gnats circling his head and, distracted, tripped over a tree root and fell to his knees. Fernando helped him up and they followed the men across a small stream, casting an eye out for snakes that Pedro imagined must be slithering under the carpet of ferns. Much more beautiful were the multicolored orchids that hung from the tall canopy of cedars.

The terrain was steep, and the path they followed was barely wide enough for a Jeep to pass. After three hours, they reached a point of descent where the track veered sharply to the east.

The men felled a cedar so that it blocked the track just after the turn. Half the guerrillas went to the left, and the other half took up positions on the right, crouching in a thick jumble of ferns and banana trees, their gun barrels trained on the road. Pedro recognized some nearby plants as medicinal, the names that his father had taught him long forgotten. Any force coming up the track would be unable to see the gauntlet of men hidden on either side. It was four o'clock in the afternoon and Pedro's shirt was soaked in perspiration, but the group waited patiently in their cramped position for three more hours, like spiders silently expecting their prey.

At first Pedro heard a faint sound, like that of a large dragonfly beating its wings. Then the noise morphed into a mechanical whirr. Pedro could see a Jeep in the distance, advancing up the road from the south. An officer sat to the right of the driver, a radioman occupying the backseat. A machine gun was anchored to a bracket at the rear of the Jeep. Behind the Jeep, two lines of regular army soldiers climbed up the track. The guerrillas let the Jeep pass through the beginning of their trap unmolested, allowing the balance of the column to come within range of their hidden guns. Mosquitos hovered near Pedro's head, but he crouched motion-ionless.

The soldiers arrived at the felled cedar and had just started to turn back when the guerrillas began firing. There was no escape. First, they shot out the Jeep's tires. The radioman attempted to fire the Jeep's machine gun, but he and the two other men in the vehicle were cut down in seconds. The rest of the column sought refuge in a ditch, but the Fidelistas picked them off fairly easily. The battle lasted less than ten minutes, and those government forces who were not dead or wounded ran off into the distance. Pedro fired his gun, but purposefully pointed it away from any target.

He thought he saw a movement in the ditch, and then he heard a shot. Colonel León, whose gun had jammed, was trying to free the bolt of his rifle. Another shot from the ditch. Next to Pedro, Fernando dropped his rifle, and fell into the road. Pedro picked up Fernando's rifle. He found the trigger and located the source of the shots. On the other side of the track, a dirty-faced, terrified soldier grasping a rifle looked up, his face contorted with pain. He pointed his gun in the direction of León. Pedro aimed carefully and pulled the trigger. His target's head disappeared. Pedro turned to Fernando, who was gripping his abdomen where blood from his wound spread across his oversized camouflage shirt. It was the color of beet juice, dark red and thick. Just like Alberto's, Pedro thought. Pedro knelt and patted Fernando's head. *The blood of Christ, shed for you*—how many times had he uttered those words offering wine during Mass? The boy opened his mouth, but before uttering a word, stopped breathing. His rifle fell from Pedro's hands.

"I have to sit down," Pedro said and slid to the ground. He turned to one side and vomited onto the ferns.

Colonel León stepped forward and put his hand on Pedro's shoulder. "Good shot, Father," he said calmly. "I think you may have saved my life."

Everyone was shouting in victory. Pedro heard the words, but not the music.

"Fernando is dead," he finally managed to mutter. "He taught me how to shoot not an hour ago."

Wild with jubilation, Dolores came running, Luis Ferrer with her. She hardly noticed Pedro's plight.

"You blew off half his head," she cried out. "We nailed those bastards, didn't we?"

Ferrer gave Pedro a slap on the back. "And our boy here died a hero of the revolution. What's done is done. Now those Batistianos in Palma Soriano have no reinforcements. That's going to be a mop-up operation. After that, there's nothing to stop us between here and Santiago."

Pedro wiped his mouth with his hand. "I'd like to get back to Havana."

"Oh no, Father," said Luis. "You must come with us to Santiago. I personally guarantee that once we take that city, you will get to your boat. Batista is finished!" He grabbed Dolores, and danced her around.

The guerrillas buried their dead and packed up the wounded of both sides. Camping for the night, Luis and his officers listened to Radio Rebelde. Che Guevara and Camilo Cienfuegos were having success in the central plains, the two hundred-mile stretch east of Havana. It was almost Christmas, and the revolution's star was on the rise.

"Father," said Dolores, putting her arm around Pedro's shoulders. "You did well today. I'm proud of you. When they write the history of the revolution, you'll have a place in it."

"I don't want a place in the history of the revolution. Priests don't kill people," he said bitterly.

"The revolution needed you, and you stood up and were counted."

Pedro remained silent.

Chapter 15

The Palma Soriano operation was hardly the "mop-up" that Luis Ferrer had predicted. But it only lasted three days and by December 27, it was over. The rebels had won with Luis commanding them. Pedro stayed out of the fighting at a coffee plantation, five miles north of town, hearing the distant sounds of battle, but relieved not to be participating. He spent all his time brooding, massaging his desperation. María at home wanting only to love him, a small sin; Dolores on the battlefront making him a hero when he loathed himself for killing, a mortal sin; his heresy in general.

For three nights, Colonel León gave Pedro succor. He reminded the anguished priest of how important the revolution was, how cruel and devious were the Batistianos. He spoke of La Cabaña—a torture chamber of innocents. He fed Pedro and supplied him with a bottle of rum. Pedro was grateful, but not comforted. A pulse in his ear throbbed continuously, a rhythmic pressure about once a second that drove him to ask for another bottle.

Pedro was attempting to relax with León on the second-floor terrace on the afternoon of December 27, when Ferrer and Dolores drove up in a captured Jeep, its horn honking madly.

Dolores gushed over the details of the battle, as if she were describing the results of a soccer game. "The best part is that we seized seven hundred fifty weapons and eighty-five thousand rounds of ammunition. Now we have enough guns to attack Santiago."

"We're meeting Fidel at Central Oriente, an abandoned sugar mill in Las Mercedes. No more trekking up and down these damned mountains on foot—the army's been wiped out, and we've got wheels!"

The Jeep squealed to a stop in front of the main building of the defunct Central Oriente, next to a green Land Rover.

I see the *Comandante en Jefe* is already here," said Luis. "He loves that Land Rover." Hundreds of soldiers stood around, their weapons holstered or slung over their shoulders.

No killing today, Pedro thought, his ear beginning to pulse again.

Out of the building appeared a familiar figure, a man who towered over the others, carrying a rifle with a telescopic sight. Despite his long hair and unkempt beard, the man was easily recognizable; it was Pedro's old classmate from the Belén School—Fidel Castro Ruz.

Fidel strode toward them and wrapped his arms around Ferrer. Close behind walked a shorter and stockier version of *El Jefe*—Raúl Castro—another familiar face from Belén. He was five years younger than Fidel and had dropped out of school to return to his father's sugarcane fields. Now, he was second-in-command to his brother.

"Congratulations, Luis," exclaimed Fidel. "So I understand that they're calling you 'the butcher.' There's nothing stopping us now."

He turned his attention to Dolores. "And how's the queen of the revolution? I hear you brought a load of machine guns to the party."

Dolores kissed Fidel on both cheeks. "You know me, I'm a party kind of girl."

Pedro felt Fidel's attention focus on him. His stare was piercing, cutting through the years. "You—you look familiar. Was it Belén or the university?" he asked with a quizzical smile. "I don't remember."

"Actually, *Comandante*, it was both," answered Pedro. He tried not to stutter. "You were quite a sportsman, as I remember."

"Not been much time for baseball or basketball in the past few years," Fidel replied, walking around Pedro as if he were surveying a store mannequin. He put his hand to his chin. "Now I remember—Pedro Villanueva. You were dating that beautiful blonde, Alicia, Norma—no, Isabel! That's it—the beautiful Isabel."

"You have a good memory, *Comandante*, but that was a long time ago," Pedro replied, memories of Isabel's rejection when he had shown no interest in joining the young Communist movement exhumed.

136

"Your classmate is now a priest," Dolores explained. "What's more, he's the captain of the sailboat that brought me and the machine guns."

"A priest! Son of a bitch! I don't believe it," exclaimed Fidel, as he stepped over and embraced Pedro. "A priest and a patriot. The Jesuits sure knew how to raise 'em right!"

"You haven't heard anything yet," said Ferrer. "Father Pedro saved Enrique León from death four days ago."

Fidel released Pedro from his hug, then drew him close again. "You're a model for the revolution! The world will soon know of your contribution."

Fidel turned to his brother. "Raúl, come shake the hand of a real hero!"

Pedro managed a smile. He was drawn into Fidel Castro's blazing orbit in spite of himself. He remembered the time at Belén when Fidel gave an hour-long tirade against a bill presented by Vidarrueta, a Communist Party Congressman, that would abolish private schools in Cuba. He heard again the sturdy teenager's forthright speech and saw his handsome face. At the time, Pedro could barely speak his own name when called on in class. Fidel's speech was quoted in *El Mundo* and all his classmates envied him. Even then, he had been destiny's child.

The reunion was interrupted by the percussive thwacking of helicopter blades chopping at the air, as a military Sikorsky landed atop four white sheets hastily prepared to designate a landing area. An army general emerged from a cloud of flying dust, and he and Fidel embraced.

Inside the sugar mill Fidel made the introductions. The general was Eulogio Cantillo, the commander of Batista's forces in Oriente Province. Pedro noted that Fidel appeared to hold the general in high esteem.

"General, I'm grateful you came," said Fidel. "Perhaps we can use some common sense to stop this bloodshed. I'm pleased that you, unlike some of the other officers of Batista's regime, are not guilty of any war crimes."

Cantillo's face blanched as Fidel said the last two words.

Fidel continued, "I know you are an honest broker."

Pedro felt the need to pray. Perhaps my sin of murder can be absolved after all, he thought, listening to the two men who held the fate of so many in their hands. Holy Jesus, it's true! The war is about to end, and I'm here to witness it.

"*Comandante*," the general began, looking up at Fidel towering above him, "It is my honor to serve our country and—oh, I almost forgot, I left something in the chopper."

The others exchanged puzzled glances, as the general darted out and returned with a box that he placed on the table next to a pot of coffee.

"One can't have coffee without this," he said, as he removed a bottle of brandy and cigars from the box, like a magician pulling a rabbit out of a hat. He poured a shot of brandy in each of the cups. The others, all except Dolores, looked lustfully at the gifts. After months of frugal rations and near starvation, they were being rewarded, and by the enemy!

But Fidel Castro was too good a leader to be lulled by presents. Immediately, he presented a list of demands to General Cantillo. The general sat quietly, sipping his drink, while Castro paced the room, lecturing him about the perfidy of the Cuban army and the urgent need for President Batista and some of his top brass to be tried as war criminals.

"They must be captured and their assets seized," Fidel insisted, his bearded face surrounded by a cloud of cigar smoke.

The general tried to explain that while Batista was prepared to leave, he wanted assurances that the structure of the army wouldn't be dismantled. The two men reminded Pedro of lions circling each other—one roaring, one watching for his chance to strike back. A tinge of envy seized him. These guys didn't find killing an extraordinary event; it was an integral part of their life.

Fidel continued his verbal onslaught; to Pedro, his demands were becoming over the top.

"Look," and he wagged his finger in the general's face, "if you want to help, tell the garrison at Santiago to surrender. That will stop the killing. Then, if you persuade them to join the revolution, we'll all march on Havana and capture fucking Fulgencio."

The general sat silent for a long time, picking up

and putting down the empty brandy bottle. No one else uttered a word, but Fidel puffed earnestly on the precious cigar. Cantillo swallowed, as if searching for an answer that would satisfy the roaring lion. This man is going to be defeated, Pedro thought.

Finally, General Cantillo replied, almost in a mumble. "That sounds reasonable, but first I have to talk to some of my senior officers. I'll fly back to Camp Colombia and tell them about the plans for Santiago."

Pedro thought the general's plan smelled like day-old fish. He waited for the brilliant tactician to refute it.

"No!" barked Fidel. "They'll arrest you when you tell them Santiago's going to be surrendered on your orders."

"But, *Comandante*, I've given my word to my officers that I'd return and inform them of my plan so they can protect themselves and their families against Batista. They're all loyal to Cuba—none of them are the butchers that helped prop up El Presidente."

The general rose from his chair. Pedro held his breath. Was he going to give up so soon?

"You're a commander. You know what it's like to make a pledge to your troops." Would this plea strike the right chord with Fidel?

Fidel paused, his right hand on his chin, two fingers tapping his cheek.

"I don't like this one bit," he burst out, "but if you've given your word, I won't make you break it. Be sure you tell them this is not some fucking coup d'état!

They're not going to hijack the revolution. When I was a schoolboy, I cried seeing the workers on my own father's farm slaving twenty-four hours a day over yucca and sugarcane, without even a plantain to eat or a drop of water for their parched throats. I tell you, this revolution belongs to those men."

The general sighed deeply. "Peace is at hand, *Comandante*."

Early the next morning, Pedro sought out Raúl Castro. He found him gratefully inhaling his first of many daily cups of coffee A good time to approach the man, Pedro thought.

"Witnessing the meeting yesterday, I think that the revolution is all but over," he began with hesitation "You heard the plans for Santiago. I want to go home."

"And miss the best part? We're about to embark on a victory march into Santiago. After that, Havana." Raúl reached into his pocket and withdrew a flask. He poured what looked like a jigger's worth into his coffee. "Now that's more like it!"

"You don't need me any longer," Pedro begged, his voice cracking.

"That's where you're wrong," Raúl corrected, looking stunned at Pedro's insistence. "The revolution will always need you."

He handed Pedro a cup of coffee. "Father, you saved Enrique's life. Truly, there's nothing I can deny you. What's mine to give is yours."

Pedro sighed in relief. "Thank you, *Comandante*."

He used the title intentionally. It was clear that Raúl basked in this appellation, and Pedro felt he had learned the virtues of maintaining favor with those in power.

Dolores popped her head out of the tent. "What's up, boys?"

"The Father wants to head back to Havana."

"Oh, that's a splendid idea Why don't I go with him?"

Pedro felt his heart skip a beat. His sins were coming back to haunt him again.

"What? You'd leave us for a priest? You, the gal who rejects the confessional? Have you two got something going? I'm sure Luis would be interested in this."

Pedro held his breath, until Raúl broke into laughter. "Sorry, Father, just having a little fun. Dolores is staying here. But as a consolation prize, here's a safe conduct letter for you signed by me. You may need it." Raúl walked away, chortling. Pedro stared at the *salvoconducto* in his hands.

"I thought you were going to faint there for a minute," Dolores said. She spun around freely, her arms outstretched like a ballerina. "Lighten up! What we had at sea was nothing more than a pelvic handshake."

Enrique León was given the task of getting Pedro back to *La Rosa Blanca*. He commandeered a Jeep, and with two guerrillas riding in the back, whisked Pedro back to Moa. What had taken them days of trudging up and down the mountain passes needed only a few hours on the central highway. The colonel took charge of provisioning the boat, while Pedro cleared the debris from the deck of *La Rosa Blanca*. In two hours, she was ready to sail.

Pedro watched the two soldiers who had accompanied them get into the Jeep. When León made no move to follow them, Pedro realized the revolution had yet another surprise for him.

"I'm going with you," León said. "Don't even bother to protest. It's been decided."

"Decided? Decided by whom?"

"By all of us. I'm not letting you sail six hundred miles by yourself."

Yes, it was the safe thing to do, Pedro thought.

"You've sailed before?"

"I've got a few races under my belt. I even crossed to Florida a few years back. I wouldn't want to do that again—those are dangerous waters."

Pedro shrugged. "You've convinced me, let's get underway."

The day faded into night, and Pedro stared at the stars in the winter sky. They twinkled like millions of lights memorializing Fernando and Alberto and each of Batista's victims. He breathed in the cool sea air. Somehow, his broken vows and many deceptions seemed less agonizing out here. Democracy had come to his country, at a great cost, but still— He recalled Fidel's sincerity that the revolution was the people's and not the generals'. This was a cause for good, a chance for Pedro to strip off his collar like a caterpillar shedding its cocoon, and assume an effective role. What that would be he had yet to learn, but he was ready to serve.

Chapter 16

Ordinarily, New Year's Eve in Havana was bustling with revelers stocking up for the evening festivities. December 31, 1958, fell on a Wednesday, and the few stores that were open in the morning were shuttered by noon. The streets were deserted. Around the hotels, which were full of foreigners, the parties were slow getting started. Patrons noticed that many of the staff were absent, and at some resorts, guests went into the kitchens to scrounge for food. In the neighborhoods, there was a ghostly calm.

Meanwhile, on their fourth day at sea, Pedro and Colonel León listened intently to the radio, trying to divine what was happening in Santiago. The first radio reports didn't mention events in Oriente Province, but instead breathlessly announced the news that many had hoped for, and a few had dreaded: before the new year was one hour old, President Batista had fled Cuba, together with his political apparatchiks and generals and their families.

Pedro was elated. He thought back over the past weeks. He asked himself again if it had been worth it.

He shouted silently to himself. Yes! For the first time in my life, I am part of something worthwhile, accomplishing something. Yes, yes, it was worth every second! Pedro let out a loud whoop and did a little jig standing at the wheel of *La Rosa Blanca*.

Best of all, he would soon see María again and rejoice in her presence. The last month had been so fraught with danger and excitement that he had put her love to one side. Now, in quietude, he remembered their last words, exchanged with the specter of uncertain death hanging over his head. Physically, at least, he had arrived back safely. But the questions were many, the answers few.

As he brought *La Rosa Blanca* up to her mooring at the club at about eight P.M., he turned off the radio. It had been rehashing every detail of the spontaneous celebrations breaking out all over Havana, as well as news of a few attacks that had occurred when rebel forces encountered Batista supporters and meted out curbstone justice. There was one piece of news that Pedro had not heard before. An excited announcer said that Santiago's Moncada garrison had surrendered, and that all of the troops had gone over to the revolution.

"I guess Cantillo came through on *one* of his promises," Pedro said to León.

Ordinarily, the club would be full of diners and dancers, but that night the club was deserted and all the doors were locked, although the members' yachts and the club Lightnings were moored as usual.

A guerrilla with the familiar long hair and bushy beard was sprawled at the entrance, out of the rain that was coming down in buckets.

Pedro asked, "Why is the club closed? Why are you here?"

"Dunno," answered the soldier. "Just following orders."

"Do you have any transport?" León asked the guard.

"Not until my sergeant comes for me."

León embraced Pedro and said farewell. "I'll stay and wait for his relief."

Pedro ran down the street to the Hotel Comodoro and phoned Tomás.

His brother arrived at the hotel within a half hour to encounter a person he did not recognize, a wet and bedraggled man in dirty fatigues and a beard. I must look pretty authentic, Pedro thought, as he spied Tomás.

"*Aquí estoy*," Pedro called out.

"Oh my God, where have you been?" asked Tomás. "You look like shit!"

"I'm delighted to see you, too," Pedro replied.

"*La Rosa Blanca* is gone, you're gone. You said you were going to Guantánamo for two weeks. It's been a month!"

"I'll tell you, but first get me home. I can't stand the way I look and smell. I want to take a bath for a week!"

Tomás sniffed the air derisively. "Sounds like a good idea to me!"

As they drove through the narrow streets of Old Havana, Tomás was full of news. "The world's been falling apart. That fanatic Castro's on his way here. I even called your friend Domingo, and he tells me that the bishop's beside himself. No one knows what to expect or where you've been!"

"Don't worry, Tomás. Everything's going to be okay. I was just with Fidel outside Santiago."

"You? Fidel? Santiago?" Tomás swerved up on a curb.

"There are some things I haven't been able to tell you. I'm sorry, but these are dangerous times. Ever since Alberto, may he rest in peace, was murdered, I've been in the M-26-7 underground."

"Holy Mother of God!" Tomás made the sign of the cross.

They arrived at Espíritu Santo. "It's true, brother," said Pedro. "There's a lot to tell, but first, a hot bath and a good sleep."

"Then you better pray for hot water. The power keeps going off. And for Christ's sake, call Mamá and Papá!"

Pedro took in all the old familiar associations of his tiny apartment, as if he'd been gone for years instead of a month—his violin in the corner, his missal on the table, Espíritu Santo outside his window standing vigil. He luxuriated in a hot bath, clean for the first time in a month, then collapsed onto the bed and slept a dreamless sleep, also for the first time in a month.

When he awoke, Pedro thought of María. But ever the dutiful son, he called his parents at once. They were relieved and angry at the same time.

"So much for going away for two weeks," Asunción said, her voice heavy with bitterness. "How can you worry us so, and so soon after Alberto's— I'm putting your father on."

Pedro had always found his father's voice reassuring. Its deep timbre had the wisdom of the ages. "I'm glad you're safe. It looks like your revolution has been successful. I take it that your trip to Guantánamo wasn't exactly as you'd planned."

Pedro hesitated.

"I just didn't want to worry you and Mamá," Pedro explained. "I've been with Fidel outside Santiago."

Pedro heard his father sigh deeply on the other end.

"I'm not surprised," his father said. "I just hope that this revolution is everything you want. Cuba has had revolutions for more than sixty years, and not one has brought us any peace of mind."

"This one's different. Fidel is different. You'll see— the terror and corruption of the Batista government are over."

Then he remembered. "Papá, why is the club closed and a guard posted at the entrance?"

"We were just arriving for dinner there two days ago, and a half-dozen *barbudos* came into the dining room and announced that the club was closed until further notice. No reasons—just 'orders of the revolution.'"

"I'm sure this is just a temporary measure," said Pedro. "I'll try to find out more."

"We love you, son. Visit when you can."

Pedro stared at the phone and hesitated. María. He thought about what he *would* say, what he *could* not say, and what he *should* not say. He dialed her number. The phone rang and rang. As he was about to hang up, María came on the line. When she heard his voice, she cried out, "You're safe! Thank God."

"Yes, I just got in."

"Isn't it wonderful—the revolution is over, and that scoundrel Batista is gone, along with his henchmen! Out!" María's voice rose in a crescendo. "I keep telling it to myself. Finally, we have our freedom back."

"Yes, it's been a long struggle."

"But why have you been gone so long? I thought you were going to deliver the guns to Oriente and then return right away."

"Sometimes things don't work out as planned. I'll tell you all about it when I see you."

"When will that be?"

"Tomorrow, I'll come for dinner. Will that be okay?"

"I can't wait! We have a lot to celebrate."

Pedro hoped that was true.

The next morning, after shaving off a month's growth of beard and having Miguel cut his hair, Pedro glanced in the mirror. Never heavy, he was now so thin that he looked haggard, despite his suntanned skin. He savored the thought of María's cooking that night. Perhaps she'll make *ropa vieja*. He picked up his violin; perhaps there would be an opportunity to play duets. The warmth of the contoured chinrest was like the caress of a lover. He adjusted the tuning pegs and tightened the horsehair in the bow. He was about to play the first notes of his favorite Mendelssohn concerto when there was a loud rap on his door. Frustrated, he put his instrument on a chair.

León burst through the door. "We've got to go!"

"Go? Why?"

"Fidel and the others are about to arrive in a caravan at Matanzas. They're with hundreds of rebels advancing on Havana."

"But what do you need of me?"

"I spoke to Raúl. He's as superstitious as a *Sántero.* He says you're his lucky charm. He wants you with him when they come into the capital."

Pedro thought of María. The idea of putting off their reunion was unacceptable. "Tell Raúl you couldn't find me."

"Don't ever think about lying to either Raúl or Fidel. You might as well shoot yourself."

"You mean I have to cancel all my plans because Raúl thinks I'm his personal horseshoe?"

"When you saved his top commander's life, don't be surprised that he thinks highly of you."

• • •

Matanzas, a town just fifty-five miles east of Havana, was known as the Venice of Cuba, with seventeen bridges over the three rivers that ran through it. When Pedro and León arrived in the town square, they found that the caravan had already occupied it. Dolores and Fidel appeared to be arguing. Raúl and Luis stood silently, looking bemused. The discussion stopped when Fidel took note that León and Pedro were there.

"Oh my God," he said as he opened his arms and gave Pedro a warm hug. "It's my triple threat—sailor, priest, guerrilla." Fidel reached up and touched Pedro's clean-shaven face.

"Well, maybe not such a guerrilla." Looking to León, he laughed at the sight of his well-trimmed beard. "It looks like you had time to clean up, too!"

Fidel turned his attention back to Dolores. "And what's the reason again for stopping here?" he demanded. "I want to get to the capital before dark."

"I don't trust any reporters, but I made some arrangements through Señor Jules Dubois of the *Chicago Tribune* for a TV star from the U.S. to interview you."

"Who's that?" asked Fidel. The revolution had taken its toll, and he looked like he hadn't slept in days.

"Ed Sullivan. He has a show on Sunday nights that everyone in the U.S. watches. Cuba has six, maybe seven million, people. When you make your first radio address, maybe you'll reach half of them. If you go on Ed Sullivan's show, you'll be able to share the story of our revolution with more than fifty million people watching in their living rooms."

Pedro was impressed by both Dolores's tenacity and her intelligence. Apparently, Fidel felt the same way, as he brightened up at her story.

"Okay, what do I have to do?" he asked.

Pedro felt like a witness to history. Here he was with the new leader of his country, the entire village of Matanzas welcoming him like the second coming of Christ. And shortly, so would the United States, thanks to Ed Sullivan.

To increase the drama, Fidel put off his interview with Ed Sullivan, whom he had taken to calling "that gringo son of a bitch," until two A.M., even though the famous entertainer and his entourage had been cooling their heels since five P.M. When the time came for the interview, Fidel, Raúl, Luis, Dolores, Pedro, and about two hundred of their cohorts, armed with rifles and pistols, filed into the provincial palace. A room there had been set up as a temporary TV studio.

"Not bad for a *'hijo de puta.'*" Pedro remembered that the epithet "whore's boy" had been used by some at Belén to refer to Fidel's illegitimacy.

Ed Sullivan, in his worsted wool suit and with his droopy eyes, looked to Pedro like an overdressed basset hound. He asked no hard questions and, in every case, gave Fidel the benefit of the doubt.

In the middle of the interview, Sullivan commented,

"I heard that your army was *Communeestah*, and that you were *Communeestah*. I've seen your army, and they wear scapulars, they wear medals around their necks, they carry bibles. Cuba, I know, is mostly Catholic, and you, too, aren't you Catholic?"

"Yes, I studied at a Catholic school," answered Fidel.

Sullivan accepted Fidel's parry without comment, and turned to the problem of Latin American dictators looting their countries and then moving on.

"How are you going to prevent that in Cuba?"

"Very simple," Fidel answered. "We're not going to permit any dictatorship. You can be sure that Batista is the last dictator of Cuba, because now we are going to improve our democratic institutions."

Sullivan concluded that Fidel was the George Washington of Cuba, announcing that belief to all the viewers back home. For their part, Fidel and the others seemed re-energized.

After the dark years in the Sierra Maestra, Pedro thought, no wonder Fidel likes the attention of the TV lights.

Chapter 17

"I'm so sorry that I disappeared again. You're not going to believe where I've been."

Pedro was apologizing to María. Not only had he missed spending the entire previous evening with her, but Dolores had also called another meeting of the Defarge Circle for that night. She had changed the name to the Free Cuba Committee, and he wondered if it had new goals.

"I never know where you are anymore, so I try not to worry."

"Sounds like a good idea," said Pedro. "And the Defarge Circle is having another meeting tonight at your house!"

"How do you know that?" she asked.

"I just left a meeting with our leaders."

"Are you joking? You and Raúl and Fidel?"

"It's been an interesting month."

"I can see that. Come early tomorrow. There's a lot to catch up on." María's voice sounded like a child expecting a present.

She really wants to see me, thought Pedro. That last embrace—it wasn't just my imagination.

Pedro dressed in his jungle fatigues for the meeting, hoping to impress María with his tan and his attire. Apparently he did, for when he walked into her house, she enveloped him in her arms. Her embrace was unguarded and powerful. "I've missed you so much," she whispered.

"Me, too," he said. "Many nights in the mountains, I imagined that you were there with me. And we have a lot to talk about. But first, I was hoping that after the meeting, we might play some duets. I remembered your Steinway and brought my violin with me."

Yes, lots of time to talk, and time for music, too, he thought. María almost made him forget that the throbbing in his ear had started up again.

The first post-revolutionary meeting of the Defarge Circle seemed more like a party than a serious affair, as the group gathered, on time for once, clinking Cuba Libres in toasts to the success of the revolution. Pedro looked at the former underground collaborators, glad to be free of the fear of Batista's secret police infiltrating their meetings and happy to be in María's company. Finally, Dolores appeared to remember the reason for the meeting. She quieted the now somewhat boisterous troops and told them she was discarding her code name.

"I've come a long way with the revolution," she explained. "I started with Raúl, Luis, and Fidel five years ago in Mexico. My father wanted me to be an engineer, but instead, I've engineered a revolution—together with you, my comrades. But there's still work to be done. I want to rename the Circle as a start."

The group all looked at one another.

"Yes, it's time to leave the antique French Revolution and embrace the modern. We're now the Free Cuba Committee. No more hiding for us!"

"But what exactly are we to do?" asked María.

"It depends," answered Dolores. "There were many in the old Batista hierarchy who opposed us. We need to know their identities. The revolution will reward its friends, but it will also punish its enemies."

"I've heard on the radio that there's looting going on in downtown Havana and elsewhere," Juan, the polo player and engineer, tentatively offered.

"Unfortunately, that's true. We need to allow some time for the discipline that our *barbudos* showed in battle to take over in the streets. The Free Cuba Committee must help spread the word that we're dedicated to eliminating the corruption of the police, as well as the government. The almighty dollar does not reign any longer." Dolores looked at each member individually and explained what she wanted of each.

"To you, María—you're the third-ranking official in El Tribunal de Cuentas. You're going to keep your job, but if you hear of any disloyal grumblings among the staff, or the people your employees audit, you're to keep me informed."

"I went into the office this past Monday, and everyone came in except for my boss, Fernandez," said María. "No one knew what to do, and we section chiefs felt like a ship without a rudder. We all got together and celebrated. We agreed that the tribunal had to get back to work as fast as we could. It's going to be wonderful operating without Batista making us do favors for his special friends."

"All government has to get back to work as soon as possible," said Dolores. "Batista stole all the wealth of the treasury. There's no time to lose."

Dolores turned to Pedro. "And Padre, I want you to stay at Iglesia del Espíritu Santo. There, you can tell us what the archdiocese is up to."

Oh my God, thought Pedro, I'm never going to escape that constricting collar. The throbbing in his ear intensified.

"But Dolores, I've no further use for the priesthood. My experience with you and the others in the Sierra convinced me that my place is now outside the church, with you. Certainly there must be a job for me somewhere."

"I'm not asking you to remain at the church forever—just for a few months until Fidel and Luis can determine whom they can trust. We have contacts in Oriente, in Santiago."

At the mention of Pedro having been in Santiago, there was murmuring from the other members of the newly christened Free Cuba Committee.

"You were in the mountains?" asked Juan. "What did you see?"

"Did you see any shooting?" asked the banker, Federico. "Did you meet Fidel? What's he really like?"

Pedro dodged the questions. He was not ready to discuss his activities in the Sierra Maestra.

"Our Pedro is a genuine hero of the revolution," said Dolores. "He saved the life of one of our top commanders and probably Raúl Castro's as well."

"Now you're going too far," Pedro demurred, scratching at his ear.

Dolores gave him a hard look. "Just stay at Espíritu Santo, and I'll be in touch."

Pedro gave a sigh of relief after everyone else had left. After another Cuba Libre, he coaxed María to play for him. She was a good pianist; he was entranced by the soaring phrases of the Emperor Concerto.

"Brava," he exclaimed. "Such talent!"

"Thank you, Father, but I have sinned," María said. "I cheated on the finale and added my own ending."

That title again. The sound of it caused Pedro to wince inwardly.

"Please María, please call me Pedro. There's no more 'Father' for us despite Dolores's instructions."

María nodded. "I guess we *have* gone beyond your title," she admitted.

"There's still much we have to learn about each other," said Pedro.

It took him two minutes to retrieve his violin from the Plymouth. Tucked inside his case was the Mendelssohn E Minor Concerto he'd rehearsed earlier in his apartment, as well as a piano accompaniment. He brought out the folio with a flourish.

María gawked at the score in front of her. "*Ave María Purísima,* you expect me to sight read this, Father—I mean—Pedro. You have too much faith in me."

Pedro started out with the melodic theme that carries through the first movement, while María studied her part as he played.

"See, you and I just plow into the theme without any introduction. I'll start slowly."

María began playing hesitatingly, but it didn't take long for her to become acquainted with the melody. When Pedro's violin rested, she took over the soaring theme of the first movement. A few moments passed and Pedro's violin began to reprise the theme as the two instruments intertwined in a passionate exchange

She stopped playing, got up from the Steinway, took his hand, and led him to the sofa. She brought her lips to his, grazing them gently.

"This was the worst Christmas of my life. But the New Year has already gotten better."

He felt her hand run down his back, caressing the muscles of his upper arm, then return to his hair. Her lips parted, her tongue found his, and their embrace became more fervent. "It's been so long," she said. "I'm not sure if I remember how this is done."

Pedro was sure they wouldn't have to worry. As he

unbuttoned María's blouse, he flashed back to Dolores and her wild, knowing groping on the deck of *La Rosa Blanca*. Before this, what intimacy he'd had with a woman was limited to Isabel's youthful gymnastics and Dolores's chaotic gyrations. At last, he understood what it meant to actually make love to a woman.

Chapter 18

Two days later, Pedro prepared for Mass at Espíritu Santo. It had been more than a month since he'd celebrated the rite, and his cassock weighed heavily on his shoulders. Two choirboys were already there with Miguel, who helped him remove his cassock and don his white vestments worn over the black gown. Ordinarily, the vestments hung loosely, but this day, the familiar garment seemed huge, as if he'd wrapped himself in *La Rosa Blanca*'s mainsail.

Domingo, who'd been filling in for Pedro in his absence, rushed in through the door. "Holy Mother of God, you're back safely!" he exclaimed, as he embraced his friend with the force of a giant wave.

Pedro allowed himself to be drowned by Domingo's outstretched arms and the folds of his voluminous robe.

"So much has happened since you went to Guantánamo," burbled Domingo. "Every day the archbishop called to ask if I knew anything about your return. And now you're back and you don't call me! What am I, a zero to the left?"

Overhead, the church bells began to chime.

"Domingo, after services, come to my apartment and I'll fill you in. Now we have other things to do," said Pedro, lighting candles for the choirboys. He took his shepherd staff, and with the choirboys leading him, proceeded into the sanctuary and up to the altar.

Amazingly, there were nearly a hundred parishioners filling the pews. God has a sense of humor, Pedro thought. When I wanted to be a priest and fill the seats, few came. Now, being a priest is the last thing I want to do, and the world comes to my door. Resigned that he needed to keep up the pretense for a bit longer, he began, *"In nomine Patris, et Filii et Spiritus Sancti."*

When Pedro returned to his apartment after Mass, he found Domingo rooting around his kitchen.

"There's nothing to eat here, either," Domingo complained. "It's no different at my place. I feel like the Israelites when they were commanded to make bricks with no straw." Domingo went from one kitchen cabinet to another, opening one, seeing it empty, then banging it shut.

"I went to the bodega, and for the first time in ages, there was nothing but rice and beans. No fresh meat, no fresh fruit or vegetables. Just this box of rice and a can of beans. How can I make *ropa vieja*?"

Pedro responded, "It's going to take some time for the new government to get things running smoothly. Fidel is a brilliant planner. I'm sure before long, the markets will be overflowing. We all must be a little patient with imperfection. We're so used to bureaucratic

163

corruption that there's certain to be some housecleaning before the government starts operating efficiently. Democracy and a free market will fix everything. We couldn't be in better hands than Fidel's."

"I was at a meeting with the archbishop yesterday," said Domingo, "and he advised that our churches should continue to focus on the religious needs of our parishioners and stay out of politics. There are rumors that Fidel is a Communist, but he has never done anything to indicate that he's not just another overachieving Catholic boy."

"When I was up in the Sierra with Luis, Raúl, and Fidel, there wasn't much going on that was at all in the Catholic tradition," said Pedro. "Although I was asked to hear the confession of one of the rebels. But Fidel is definitely not a Communist. He told me that the Communist Party is a debating society for old men." Pedro wondered about confessing his own sin of taking a life, but decided not to risk his friend's wrath or pity.

"What? You spoke to Fidel? I heard that you'd just taken a couple of weeks off in Guantánamo after your brother died."

"I couldn't tell the archdiocese where I was going for security reasons."

"Hmm. It's not good to lie to the bishop."

"I had no choice." Pedro almost laughed in Domingo's face, thinking about what a liar he'd turned out to be.

"One always has choices."

"War turns our conventional perception of morality

on its head. What seems like a logical and moral choice in the comfort of Havana can have deadly consequences in combat."

Domingo shook his head in disapproval. "Don't start to lecture me about relative morality. There are sins that aren't negotiable—lying, killing, adultery—those are absolutely wrong. War or no war."

Domingo finished preparing the rice and beans and brought them to the table. He went to a cupboard and pulled out a bottle of wine and two glasses. "I think we both could use some fortification."

He struggled with the corkscrew and managed to extract the cork from the bottle. He poured two glasses of claret. Inhaling the vapors of wine deeply, he took a sip.

"You look troubled, my friend. The mountains must have been very difficult for you."

"I've seen things and done things that I never thought I could do, and they're not things that any priest should ever do."

Pedro relished the chance to say what he'd been feeling since he'd embarked on his voyage to Moa. As his words poured out, he felt the pulse in his ear stop throbbing. He took a deep breath.

"I don't see how I can remain a priest any longer. I need advice."

"I'm honored, my friend, but I wish I could serve it up with some meat. One can't discuss such weighty subjects without protein. At least a little chicken would be nice—"

Pedro interrupted Domingo's descent into alimentary concerns. "Did you ever feel you made a mistake? That being a priest wasn't the right profession for you?"

Pedro looked away from Father Domingo as he asked this last question. He would undoubtedly be shocked to his fat little core.

"So what's her name?"

Pedro stared at Domingo in disbelief. "Who said anything about a 'her'?"

"Pedro, the flesh of a donkey is not transparent, but you—I can see right through you. I know every line and dimple in your face, and I know you don't have any deficits in your understanding of the liturgy. And I've seen you do more Masses than I care to remember. So I ask myself, what could be causing one of my best students, one of the best of the young generation of priests, to question if he should be a priest, and I say to myself 'Domingo, who is the woman?'"

Pedro breathed a sigh of relief.

Domingo seemed unfazed. "How long have you questioned yourself about this?"

"Longer than I can remember."

"And have you ever spoken to anyone about your feelings before?"

"No."

"Then I ask you again. Who is the woman?"

Finding no way to deflect Domingo's cross-examination, Pedro plowed ahead. "She's a widow, a mother of three, and a high official at El Tribunal de Cuentas. She is stunningly beautiful. I love the sound of her voice and the tilt of her head as she listens to me. When I'm with her, all seems right with the world."

"Is she religious?" Domingo asked.

"I doubt that she can remember the last time she's been to church."

"And what do you want to do about this woman?"

"I want to spend my life with her, and yet with everything I've seen and done, and what this means about the vows that I have taken to the church, I feel paralyzed and unworthy of her."

"And how does she feel about you?"

"Before I went to the Sierra Maestra, she told me that she loved me. And I told her that I loved her, too. Just two days ago, we—"

"My dear Pedro, the city is being looted. Fidel and his Neanderthals are on every major street corner as if hunting for wild animals. Houses and businesses are being broken into; the Fidelistas are executing Batistianos at breakneck speed."

Pedro paced the floor. Domingo's sudden change of subject was disconcerting. "The times are certainly unsettled. But Fidel has been making speeches on the radio, reminding his guerrillas that they are soldiers and are expected to follow orders, and that his orders are clear—no looting. I believe he's serious, and his followers will get under control."

Pedro looked at Domingo and sighed deeply. "Forget the revolution. What about me? I asked you a question!"

Domingo took another helping of rice and beans.

167

After a satisfying belch, he continued, "Pedro, you're a good man. Meditate on this. Think it through. Find the divine spark that's deep inside you, and you will then do God's will." Domingo poured himself another glass of claret.

"Now, it is God's will that we finish this bottle of excellent wine."

Over the next hour, Pedro and Domingo managed to empty the bottle. Pedro entertained Domingo with his meeting with Fidel in the Sierra Maestra. Domingo, though dismissive of Cuba's new leader, nevertheless urged Pedro on and even seemed a bit jealous when he was told about *The Ed Sullivan Show* and Pedro's part in it. As for the mortal sin Pedro had committed for the revolution, he was sure Domingo wasn't ready to hear his confession about that just yet.

Their reunion was interrupted by a knock on Pedro's door. A *barbudo* carrying a machine gun strapped to his back stood at the threshold. "Are you Father Pedro Villanueva?" he asked.

Pedro identified himself.

"Father, I have a message from my *comandante*."

The guerrilla handed Pedro a white envelope. The note was handwritten and to the point:

> *Father, please accompany this comrade to La Cabaña immediately. A highly visible police official is our prisoner. We want to make a great showing by providing him the last rites. Luis in-*

sists that you're the only one for the job. The public must be shown that the new government believes in religious freedom, and there is no better way than to have the priest, who is a hero of the revolution, be seen providing comfort to a condemned man.

—Dolores Barré

"I'm no hero," Pedro mumbled to Domingo, who was snoring on the sofa, and, not for the first time, wondered why the leaders of M-26-7 chose to treat him like one. "Just your ordinary, everyday heretic hypocrite."

A large crowd surged around the entrance to La Cabaña when Pedro arrived in a Jeep driven by the messenger. Trucks from CMQ TV6 surrounded the building, and cables ran every which way like an assembly of giant snakes. This was a much bigger production than the Ed Sullivan interview, which managed with only a small film crew. Hundreds of newsmen and photographers milled about the prison, giving it a circus atmosphere. Pedro thought of the last time he'd been there, when the prison had looked like a morgue.

Dolores was sitting in a small room off the entrance in front of a desk where Che Guevara was cleaning a disassembled machine gun. A cartridge belt hung from the back of his chair. "Father, I'd like to introduce the hero of Santa Clara, Dr. Che Guevara."

"Congratulations, *Comandante,* I've heard of your

great success," Pedro said. He had heard that this young commander was afraid of nothing and had been one of the original *Granma* rebels who came from Mexico with Fidel.

"And you're the priest who saved León's life. He can't stop talking about you. A lucky shot can make you go far in the revolution."

Pedro took note of Che's singsong, unmistakably Argentinean, accent. It suggested a southern laziness, a lack of seriousness, a stark contrast to the dark implications of his words.

"We have a big fish for you today, Father," said Dolores.

"Who's the prisoner?" asked Pedro, as he looked out the office window to the chaotic scene of the yard.

"Colonel Cornelio Rojas, the former chief of police of Santa Clara."

"I've never heard of him," said Pedro. "What was he convicted of?"

"Father, he was the chief of police under that dog Batista," said Dolores. "We didn't need a trial for him."

"Everyone deserves a trial," Pedro said quietly.

"Father, please. People will think you're a counter-revolutionary."

She glared at him and at Che, who was not listening, busy lighting a cigar and laughing with a guard. In the "cage," a twelve-by-twelve-foot cell, Colonel Rojas, a stocky man in his fifties, mostly bald, sat on the floor in a filthy white shirt and dark trousers.

"Let's get this over with, Father. We each have roles to play. You do yours and I'll do mine."

The colonel gave him a grim smile. Pedro admired the officer's composure. whereas he felt frightened and tentative himself. He took his time pulling his purple stole from his pocket and draping it over his shoulder. Trembling, he sprinkled a few drops of anointing oil on the colonel's forehead. "Do you wish to confess, my son?"

"I have made my own confession to God. I have nothing further to confess to you, Father. Ask the Fidelistas what my crimes were. "

Pedro made the sign of the cross. "May the Lord Jesus Christ protect you and lead you to eternal life."

The door of the cell opened.

"Wait, I can't do this without my hat," the colonel said. He reached for his battered straw hat, put it on his head at a jaunty angle, and walked out of the cell behind one of the guards. Pedro followed. The group proceeded to the yard where bullet holes and bloody rivulets covering one wall gave evidence of recent executions. Above, on the roof line, a dozen black birds sat vigil.

In the distance, the TV camera stood waiting, its red light, like the angry eye of a Cyclops, staring without compassion at the proud man who stood defiant before the wall, the dreaded *Paredón*. Hundreds of photographers and reporters were assembled behind the firing squad. Pedro stood with the crowd of onlookers as the colonel first saluted the firing squad, bringing his right hand to the brim of his hat, then crying out, "Take the revolution, she is yours. Protect her!"

Was this man any better or worse than any other police chief, Pedro thought, his knees weak. What good did I do here and why did I do it?

Commanding his own death, Colonel Rojas shouted at the firing squad, "Take aim, one—two—three—fire!"

The colonel's hat flew into the air as rifle shots rang out; his body crumpled to the ground. The reports echoed off the blood-stained wall behind him, as the birds flew off the roof and toward the colonel's body.

The gruesome scene gave Pedro pause on the drive home. It was further proof that as a churchman, he was more useless than anyone. The church just sat there, observing convention, ignoring life's cruelties, not getting involved. It had done nothing when Batista's secret killings took place in dark alleys and dank cells far from public view, or now when the revolution's firing squad did its work under the bright lights of national television. La Cabaña is not a symbol of treachery; I am.

Chapter 19

CHIEF OF POLICE EXECUTED FOR CRIMES AGAINST HUMANITY, blared the front page of *Bohemia*. Pedro turned the page. He remembered the bravery of Colonel Rojas, his stoicism in the face of death. And there was his own uselessness. That trait must change, he vowed. He was more hopeful when he read that Fidel had given a speech at Camp Columbia, and when he concluded, it appeared that Heaven itself had ordained him leader. Castro had focused on justice and liberty, commodities that had been in short supply when Batista was head of state.

Pedro tried to put away thoughts of Alberto and Colonel Rojas, and their useless deaths. Hopefully, there would be fewer executions. He was determined to try, like María, to take Fidel at his word, to understand, as Dolores never tired of pointing out, that some sacrifices must be made.

But the news reports made it hard for him to keep on message. On Channel 6 that night, Pedro listened as fifteen thousand people jammed into Havana Sports Palace to observe the trial of Jésus Sosa Blanco, a former Batista officer in charge of the Holguin garrison. For most of the night, the manacled defendant sat onstage, bombarded by repeated shouts from the audience.

"Kill him, kill him! *¡Paredón! ¡Paredón!*"

The waning days of winter were cool. Habaneros dragged out their sweaters. On Radio Rebelde, Fidel announced that elections should be deferred for two years to give opposition political parties a chance to develop, and Pedro wasn't sure why Fidel hadn't made himself president of Cuba. Instead, Manuel Urrutia had taken the oath of office as president. José Miró Cardona was sworn in as prime minister.

Pedro's mood was turbulent; he was still carrying a load of guilt about his activities in the revolution, combined with feeling that the sense of mission he had witnessed in the Sierra Maestra was being replaced by routine governance that he was not a part of and did not understand. When he received a call from María that Dolores had requested another meeting of the Free Cuba Committee, he was glad for any excuse to be involved again, to see María. He arrived at the meeting an hour early, violin in hand. The lovers entertained themselves with a new piece with which she was unfamiliar: "Kol Nidre."

"How did you learn about Jewish music?" María asked. "From a Jewish friend?"

"No, I don't know any Jewish Cubans. My world is circumscribed. When I was a boy, my parents sent me to a music camp at Interlochen, Michigan. That's where I learned the score. It's a hauntingly beautiful accompaniment to a prayer that pleads with God to forgive us for promises we made to Him but didn't keep. It's sung on the eve of the Day of Atonement, the holiest day of the year for Jews, when they believe that God decides who will live and who will die."

"I've never heard of it," said María.

The music started peacefully, almost like a reflection. Soon it began to soar. Pedro played the melody broadly. Then the music flew to its upper registers, and when the piece concluded after about ten minutes, they were both drained of all energy.

Pedro felt that this woman with her sweet, Madonna-like face and special talent for music was a gift that he'd never expected to receive. He raised his arm to embrace her, but instead of responding, she moved from the piano to the door. Dolores and León had arrived.

"You old salt, what are you doing here?" León inquired.

"Enrique, you know the Father?" María asked, astonished.

Pedro was astonished, too. "You two have met?"

"In the army, before I joined the rebels, I had a lot of experience with accounting issues, so Luis thought it would be a good idea for me to keep an eye on El Tribunal de Cuentas," explained León.

"We live in a small world," said Pedro.

"Our comrade here is quite a sailor," said León to María. "And not a bad marksman!"

"Marksman?" asked María. "He has really not told me much about the Sierra Maestra."

"He's much too modest for his own good," replied Enrique. Pedro shot and killed one of the Bastianos just as he was about to shoot me! Then he remembered, "Luis, too!"

María turned to face Pedro. "And you never said a word to me. A priest is the last person I could imagine as a killer."

Pedro heard something like contempt in her voice. "It was not one of my prouder moments," he said.

María went on. "We of the underground certainly did what we could, but people like Pedro and me had it relatively easy. Whereas, you people," and she included Dolores and León in an expansive gesture, "risked your lives on the front lines for years."

Pedro was stung to hear his efforts described as meager. Killing was a sin for him, and there was nothing easy about living with his guilt. Nor was it easy lying to his father to get the medicine that the revolution needed. Watching his brother die in the street was not particularly easy to get over, either. Pedro wondered why María was so quick to disparage what he'd been through and fast to praise the colonel.

Chapter 20

The following day, Pedro decided that a sail would wipe the cobwebs from his head. For the first time since he'd returned from the Sierra Maestra, he wore his sailing garb instead of his cassock—an HYC polo shirt under a windbreaker. María had responded to his invitation, a good sign.

Uniformed rebels lounged on street corners, their red-and-black M-26-7 armbands ringing the sleeves of their fatigues. Military vehicles of all sorts passed busily throughout the city, small red-and-black flags flying from radio antennas. As Pedro passed through one business district, he saw that a crowd had broken into a closed shoe store and made off with all the shoes. Here and there groups in twos and threes struggled down the streets carrying TVs in their heavy wooden cabinets. Nearby soldiers appeared not to notice.

Pedro wondered about two things: why were the shops closed and why wasn't Fidel's government policing the city better?

When he turned onto Santa Catalina, leading to

María's neighborhood, the street was quiet, but littered with trash. A *fritas* restaurant and ice cream parlor that María's children loved was dark, its storefront window shattered. On Juan Bruno Zayas Street he spotted María, wearing slacks and a sweater. As always, his spirits lifted at the sight of her. Today is a day off, he thought, a chance to just be a couple in love. But he could not help but notice an unhappy cast to her usually placid face.

"Let's go," she said. "Before the children grab you."

They drove in silence past the spires of Iglesia de los Pasionistas de la Víbora and into the business district, where they were stopped behind a jam-up of cars. After crawling along for ten minutes, they reached a military roadblock. Rebel soldiers were checking identity cards.

"Where are you two lovebirds off to today?" one soldier asked Pedro suspiciously.

"We're going sailing on my boat," he replied.

"You don't have a boat anymore, comrade," said the soldier sternly. "All such rich man's toys belong to the people now. Let me see your papers. And that chiquita next to you—I want her papers, too." The soldier leered at María. "And maybe her phone number. Perhaps you'd like to spend the night with a real man, not some sailor-boy, huh, chiquita?"

Pedro withdrew an envelope from his pocket and handed it to the soldier.

"Didn't you hear me? I said I wanted your identity card!" shouted the soldier. Another soldier next to him slid the bolt of his carbine, putting a bullet in the chamber with a frightening clack.

Pedro glared at the soldier. "Just open the envelope, please."

The soldier tore open the envelope and read the brief statement that was written out above the signature of Raúl Castro. He snapped to attention.

"I'm sorry, sir, please forgive me," he said and handed the message back to Pedro. "Where do you want to go?"

"The Havana Yacht Club," answered Pedro.

"Not for much longer," the soldier could not resist saying. "I hear it is going to be a military vehicle center. But for now, Juan and I will lead the way."

"What was in the envelope?" asked María, breaking a prolonged silence that seemed to be caused by more than fear.

"Just a little insurance policy," said Pedro.

The club was deserted. A piece of plywood was nailed to the door with the words *Cerrado Por M-26-7* scrawled in red paint. Pedro felt a sense of loss, one more thing from his life no longer in order. But access to the dock was controlled by the same lock as always, and Pedro's key still worked. Onboard *La Rosa Blanca*, Pedro raised the mainsail and the jib, took a seat at the wheel, and watched María go forward and release the mooring line. She's going to make a fine sailor, Pedro thought. She learns fast. The sloop danced across the water, as the sails filled with the five-knot breeze. Pedro told himself that nothing could be more comforting to the soul than a balmy breeze shared with the woman one loved.

But it was clear that something was troubling María. Having not uttered a word since arriving at the dock, at the second buoy out of the harbor María finally found her voice. Her words tumbled out.

"Every time Radio Rebelde reported a battle in the mountains, I worried that you were dead."

She appeared to try to fashion her words appropriately before continuing. What she finally said sent ice into Pedro's veins.

"When you finally came back safe, I made a mistake in carrying on what we had started before you left. It was wrong to tell you that I loved you. I shouldn't have made love with you. I was selfish, pretending you were just an ordinary man. You aren't; you're a priest, a churchman with certain vows. The Church isn't part of my life. But I respect those for whom it is important and particularly those who serve. I can't continue this charade. It's morally wrong for me to force you to stray."

She was choking back tears. Pedro looked at the clouds signaling a weather change for the worse. Same here, he thought, and handed her a handkerchief.

"María, my dearest, I've said time and again that I'm not much of a priest. I don't think that I was meant to be a priest."

"You wouldn't be saying these things if not for me—"

"No," Pedro interrupted. "You have nothing to do

with it. I was unhappy before I met you. I love you, I love you, I love you."

"If you were so unhappy, why didn't you leave the Church before?" María shifted her seat away from Pedro.

"I became a priest at the urging of my parents, and I now see that I should never have allowed that to happen. What counts is that I love you, and I want to marry you."

"That's only how you think you feel. I made it too easy for you to say that. This is my fault, and I cannot accept the responsibility for making you leave the priesthood."

"I'm going to do it now—simply quit. Leave. Adios. No longer be a priest."

"That's the whole point of what I'm saying. I feel too guilty. I can't be responsible for your changing your entire life. You'll blame me later."

Pedro turned stubborn. "But I'm going to quit anyway."

"Quit, don't quit, it makes no difference," María's voice started to rise. The tears were gone. "Pedro, this isn't going to work out between us, even though you want it to."

Pedro heard in one sentence all his fantasies of being with María forever fall from the sky like a torn kite. He cranked the wheel hard and came about. He wasn't sure he could answer her harsh words without crying himself. "Now, what?" he choked out.

"Nothing in particular. But look, we have a new

world in which to live. A new Cuba with freedom for all. Perhaps that will be some comfort to you."

María reached out her hand to touch Pedro's on the wheel. "I'm so sorry."

He shook off her hand, turned the wheel, and headed back to shore. In the Plymouth, he stepped hard on the accelerator.

"You're sorry? You're worse than Dolores! At least she doesn't pretend that sex implies something larger. You pretended that making love meant a great deal, and that's dishonest. Even the whores outside the Havana Riviera are honest with their customers!"

The car's tires squealed as they accelerated around a curve in the road.

María grabbed for the passenger door and struggled to push it open. "What do you know about Dolores's sex life? I may be dishonest, but you're no priestly role model, either; you're a hypocrite."

"What the hell are you doing, trying to kill us?" Pedro screamed, bringing the car to a screeching halt.

María's face was stony. Pedro realized he'd overstepped, but there was no point in apologizing. What's done is done.

María responded to the sudden silence by turning on the radio. The station was playing "*Nosotros*":

> We, who love each other so much,
> Should go our separate ways,
> Don't keep asking anymore,
> It isn't because I don't love you,

I love you with all my soul,
I swear I adore you and,
In the name of this love,
and for your own good, I say good-bye.

María reached for the knob to change the station,
but Pedro pushed her hand away.

"I want to hear this!" he said.

Chapter 21

The turmoil of the first few months of revolutionary government seemed to settle down into a mechanical form of governance. By April the newspapers shifted their focus from the capture and execution of Batistianos to the more mundane business of government— putting food on the table and making sure that the power grid was operational. At Dolores's urging, Pedro remained in his position at Espíritu Santo, but each day he felt he was sinking deeper into an ecclesiastical hole from which he could never climb out. Daily rainfall made the already torrid air more humid, as if nature were sympathizing with him.

His parents lived in a limbo of dullness and grief. Domingo had taken some time off to visit his cousin in Santiago. The only bright spot in Pedro's life was León, with whom he stayed in close contact. Since León worked at María's office, he often offered news about her. Thoughts of María and her rejection were never far from Pedro's mind, but he was too proud to ask about her. It was worse than if she'd died, because with her alive across town seeing León on a daily basis,

Pedro's frustration percolated. She didn't want him, and he felt like the walking dead.

But one evening, his parents showed up at Espíritu Santo unannounced.

"We're taking you to dinner," Asunción informed him. "Ever since you came back from the Sierra Maestra, your head has been in the clouds, and we never see you. You also look as if you haven't eaten since you left home."

"I'm not in the mood for food," he complained.

"I can see that." She looked him over critically. "And none of those jungle fatigues. Papá is taking us to the Hotel Nacional. Do I have to dress you myself?"

Hugo gazed at his son, a bemused look on his face. "You better listen to her—she means it."

Pedro hadn't the strength to argue with his mother when she was in her iron-will mode. He changed into a clean cassock and climbed into the backseat of his father's Cadillac.

The Hotel Nacional de Cuba had been built in 1930, and was eight stories of white stone crowned by two ornate towers suggestive of a European cathedral. Where five months earlier the men in the dining room would have all been in tuxedoes, tonight the leaded-glass crystal chandeliers shone down on bushy-bearded Fidelistas in their military fatigues. They appeared to be drinking lemonade.

Dr. Hugo turned the talk to politics. Hugo asked, "What do you make of this Manuel Urrutia who's our new president?"

"I hear he's a well-respected judge," said Pedro. "I really don't know him, but I suspect that Fidel is pulling the strings."

Hugo turned his palms upward in doubt. "Our government is changing so often it's like a baseball game. You can't tell the players without a scorecard."

Pedro's mood brightened. Fidel would appreciate being compared to a baseball player, since he once was.

"Thank God all that firing-squad business is over," said Hugo. "Everyone was afraid to turn on the TV. I don't want to hear the word *paredón* again. I read that the executions scared a lot of people into leaving."

"Especially since it's mostly foreigners and some Batista underlings." Pedro knew he sounded scornful.

"We're better off without them. And soon there will be elections." The truth was, Pedro knew no more about the new government than his father.

"All you men like to talk about is politics," complained Asunción. "How about talking about *when-you-think-a-waiter-might-arrive*. We've been waiting twenty minutes without even a menu!"

"Mamá, that's the price of revolution. In a democracy, everyone's equal. I don't think this place still has a headwaiter," said Pedro.

"Then I'm not sure democracy is everything it's cracked up to be," said Asunción. "I like it that my telephone bill is cheaper now that IT&T is out, but there's still no food at the bodegas. It was smart of me to buy some cases of canned goods before Batista left."

"Well, I read that Fidel's off in Washington seeking

economic support," said Hugo. "He's being greeted by enthusiastic crowds wherever he goes. Hopefully, he'll come back with some aid, and the economy will start working again."

"Right now I wish Fidel would show up with a menu," Asunción fired back. "We're only here because I heard they're still serving tournedos with hollandaise sauce."

Leave it to my mother, Pedro thought, to reduce the challenges of a revolution to ordering dinner. "What would I do without you?" he asked, and hoped she was right about the menu.

Domingo returned from his holiday, and dropped by, possibly to see if Pedro had access to some tastier food than rice and beans. Pedro was playing "Kol Nidre" on his violin. For accompaniment, an LP played on his phonograph.

"Sorry, I don't want to interrupt you," said Domingo. "But what's in your cupboard?"

"Take a look," Pedro replied, returning his violin to its case. Domingo's visits were never brief.

"I love Jewish music," said Domingo.

"Actually, it was written by Max Bruch, a Christian."

"Well, he should have been Jewish. They know how to eat—chopped chicken liver, matzoh balls, brisket, honey cake. If I couldn't be Cuban, I'd like to be Jewish."

He closed the cupboard door. "Nothing here but

rice. No wonder you're so thin. That's the problem with this revolution—the markets are empty. Nobody's doing any work. We seem to be drifting—where?"

"Don't you read the paper?"

Pedro knew he sounded querulous. "Just yesterday, Fidel signed a law that's going to redistribute the land to two hundred thousand poor workers. Before you know it, they'll be producing more food than even you can eat." Pedro playfully padded Domingo's belly, its girth undiminished.

Pedro's attention was interrupted by the sound of squealing brakes on the street below. Parked at the curb of the cobblestones was a Jeep, with the familiar face of Enrique León looking up at him.

Pedro introduced León to Domingo as the soldier who'd been with him in the mountains and who was currently using his expertise in accounting at El Tribunal de Cuentas.

Domingo was gracious, almost fawning. "The revolution has been traumatizing, and we're all so glad Father Pedro returned safely."

"Pedro did a major service for his country." León placed a hand on Pedro's shoulder. "And Fidel himself asked me to tell you that he wants to formally present you with a Hero of the Revolution Medal. Since Raúl was present and witnessed your heroism, he's insistent that you be the recipient of the first award."

Pedro shook his head slowly. " I didn't go to the mountains to win bangles."

"Father, you risked your life to deliver supplies to

the revolution. In the course of this work, you saved lives—and we're grateful."

"León, I just don't see it that way. What I did was to save my own life, no one else's."

"What are you two talking about?" asked Domingo. "Who did you save?"

"Domingo, please." Pedro gave his old friend an irritated look as León interrupted.

"Just think about it. I don't have to tell anyone just yet how you feel."

"Okay, but no promises," said Pedro. "But before you leave, would you please inform us why the yacht clubs are all closed. I thought the government wanted business to resume as usual. Why are the Havana Yacht Club and the Biltmore boarded up?"

"They're symbols of a different era in Cuban history. It takes time to turn the ship of government in a new direction. Be patient, they'll be open soon."

"One of the soldiers guarding the club said it was going to be used for truck storage. I wish it could be a public boating facility. I'd like to teach young kids the joys of sailing."

"Good idea," said León as he walked to the door. "Patience."

Domingo commented, watching the back of the soldier depart, "At least the revolution seems to be leaving the Church alone."

Chapter 22

It had been a long, hot summer in Havana. After an article describing Pedro's adventures running guns to the Sierra Maestra appeared in *Vanguardia Obrera*, a publication of M-26-7, word had spread among his parishioners that Fidel regarded him as one of the heroes of the revolution. Now when he celebrated Mass, the pews were filled to overflowing. A local celebrity in the streets of Old Havana, Pedro could not help but reflect that when he did his priestly job, his parishioners stayed away. When he was being lauded for the wrong reasons, he got a churchful.

Yet, he still stuck close to the precincts of Espíritu Santo. *La Rosa Blanca* remained tethered to her mooring, never once under sail since Pedro's last abbreviated voyage with María. After Mass one Sunday at the end of August, Domingo confronted the priest, collapsed into an armchair with a disconsolate demeanor.

"I look at you and wonder if somebody died," Domingo said, resting a hand on Pedro's shoulder. "With the world beating a path to your door, and many more pesos in the coffers, you should be happy. Instead you look like the loneliest man on the planet."

"I'm no hero. I'm a hypocrite. I'm not doing what I want, and what I want I can't be doing. How would you feel?"

"I think you need a change of scenery. A cousin has given me the keys to an old house on the beach at Tarará. Why don't you come with me and we'll swim in that gorgeous water. It will do you good. You're too thin and pale."

Pedro considered the offer. The last time he had been near Tarará he saw only its lights from the deck of *La Rosa Blanca*, as they headed to the Sierra Maestra in the dead of night. With him had been Dolores and a hold full of ammunition and automatic weapons.

"Are you sure you want such a gloomy face intruding into your holiday?"

"As long as you bring a box of Sister Rosa's *pastelitos* with you, you'll be most welcome."

A rusty, wrought-iron gate guarded the front of the small, mustard-colored stucco house. A scraggy lawn of arid Bermuda grass led to the main entrance, whose weathered door creaked when opened. But the view out the sliding glass door in the back was priceless. The surf broke less than a hundred yards away, across a white sandy beach. On the patio, huge terra-cotta pots of pink bougainvillea framed the view of azure waves.

"Who did you say owns this place?" Pedro asked.

"A cousin who has emigrated to the States. We're not sure if he's coming back, but in the meantime, he left the keys with me, to use whenever I need to get away from the city. Think of it as a place to recharge your batteries."

Pedro wasted no time. He quickly donned his swimming suit, sprinted across the beach, and dove into the warm aqua translucence. Within ten minutes Domingo, still in cassock and sandals, waddled onto the beach carrying a picnic basket.

"Can't relax without sustenance," he said. "Nothing like a triple-decker club sandwich to set the mind at ease."

Pedro emerged from the ocean famished. As the two men ate and drank, shielded from the sun by a mostly dead giant pawpaw tree, Pedro reflected, "The ocean is magnificent. This is the next best thing to sailing."

He was reminded of his friend, Colonel León, hard at work at El Tribunal de Cuentas in the summer heat.

"Could I invite my friend Enrique to join us tomorrow? He's the colonel who returned with me from the Sierra Maestra."

"The more, the merrier!" exclaimed Domingo. "It will be intriguing to hear the war stories of a real revolutionary. Tell him to bring a bottle of rum, and we can toast M-26-7 with Cuba Libres."

The following afternoon, Domingo had a chance to listen to the tales of more than one real revolutionary, because Enrique León showed up accompanied by Dolores Barré and Luis Ferrer. They brought rum, wine, and in a gesture guaranteed to win the heart of Domingo, an entire beef tenderloin. Domingo looked hungrily at the gift.

Cradling the beef like a baby, he announced, "This must weigh ten pounds!" He sniffed it, and hurriedly put it in the refrigerator. "It's nice to know people in high places."

Luis and Dolores had married at the end of January at the insistence of Fidel, who wanted the leaders of the government to set high moral standards for the community—no more "living in sin," was Dolores's explanation to Pedro. "And it wasn't a church wedding," she teased, reminding Pedro of their first lunchtime conversation.

On the palm-frond-covered patio facing the sea, they consumed three bottles of wine as the afternoon wore on. León started a long-winded tale about his buddy Frank País, who had organized underground cells of labor resistance to Batista.

"Frank País was a real hero," said León. "I wish he'd lived to see what's happening today."

"Some revolutionaries get too big for their britches," said Dolores, examining the near-empty bottle of 1950 Château Pavie. "Domingo, it looks like you have a taste for Bordeaux."

"My child, an excellent wine, if I must say so," said Domingo, beaming. "Wherever did you find it? I can't find milk some days."

"It's easy to find good wines," chortled Luis. "All you need is to liberate the right wine cellar. If I'm not mistaken, this case came from the Hilton where Fidel first set up headquarters back in January."

León refused to leave the subject of Frank País. He sloshed his cup filled with wine into the air in a gesture of tribute. "I've known Frank since we were kids. He was loyal to a fault."

"Sure," said Dolores," her voice rising. "He was forming a gang that was loyal to him, not the revolution."

"No! You're wrong about Frank, Dolores," said León. He gave the woman a stony-faced glare.

Dolores reciprocated. Pedro knew how obdurate Dolores could be, but he had to admit she looked good in her skimpy bikini.

"He was devoted to Fidel to the end," León went on stubbornly. They were all a little drunk.

"The people of Santiago would have been there for us in any case," said Dolores, refusing to let the matter drop.

"Some Judas brought the Batistianos down on him," said León.

"Well, we'll never know, will we, my friend?" asked Luis, stepping in as peacemaker. "Enough talk about Frank País. Best to talk about the living."

Domingo changed the subject. "It must have been very frightening for all of you up there in the mountains."

Luis responded. "For me, the mountains were our friend and our home. When the Batistianos came after us, it was like shooting fish in a barrel."

"That's not what I remember," Dolores said. "I recall that you were such a bad shot you couldn't hit a coconut if you were standing under it."

Now, Pedro was sure Dolores had had too much to drink.

"Let me tell you about our lives in the Sierra Maestra and Mr. Sharpshooter's skill with a gun. It was mid-June of last year, and I was trekking up the mountains on a wretched trail, rutted with car tracks. It wound like a snake, full of switchbacks, blocking my view beyond the curve. The moment I heard the sound of a diesel motor, I leapt into the brush and hid in the dense growth—"

"For Christ's sake, I don't want to hear that story again," Luis interrupted, earning him a scowl from his wife.

"You must have been scared to death," said Domingo incredulously.

"In the jungle, you do what you have to do. But unlike this sharpshooter I'm married to, I never thought it was my friend. To the contrary—"

"Somebody, change the subject," begged Luis, rolling his eyes.

Pedro began to turn a corkscrew into a fourth bottle of wine.

"Speaking of sharpshooting," interrupted León,

"let me tell you about our friend here with the corkscrew. If there's anyone here who's a good shot, it's him."

"What do you mean?" asked Domingo. "Father Pedro's a marksman?"

"He had to be," Dolores chimed in. "Otherwise León would have been one dead Cuban."

Pedro heard his worst fears realized. More talk about death and his part in it.

"Yes," said Luis, slurring his speech, "Pedro shot one of those son of a bitch Batistianos before he put one into Enrique."

Pedro put down the corkscrew and turned toward the sea. "Time for a swim," he said. "Let's all go."

He gestured toward the beckoning waters. Together with Luis and Dolores, he bolted for the waves, as León and Domingo drained the last of the Bordeaux.

"I see the sharks didn't get you," said León, when the three returned to the patio. "I want to get back to Frank País for a moment. I never finished making my point."

Dolores sighed deeply. "If you must, Enrique, but you're trying my patience."

"We all need to remember that when Fidel and Raúl went to jail after the attack on Moncada Barracks in '53 and then hightailed it to Mexico with the others—"

"You know, I was one of those 'others' you're referring to—just to set the record straight," interrupted Dolores.

"Well, think of it, if it weren't for Frank País working the underground cells in Oriente until 1956, there wouldn't have been a revolutionary movement for you to join when you returned."

Pedro thought it was dangerous for Enrique to argue with Dolores. Apparently, so did Luis.

"Enrique, enough of this. We're not going to settle the debate this afternoon," said Luis.

Dolores was fuming. Pedro wondered if she knew more about the death of Frank País than she was letting on. Without Luis's calming influence, would she and León come to blows?

"I'm going for a swim again," he announced in desperation. "Who's with me?"

Dolores was not mollified. Reluctantly, she followed Pedro towards the sea, stumbling as she rose, but refusing to give up her stubborn point of view.

"Nice little villa you have here, Padre," she shot at Domingo, "but the revolution needs places like this for the workers."

Chapter 23

It was nearing the end of October. Following Dolores's
advice, Pedro had bided his time as a priest in Espíritu
Santo, taking some comfort in the increased attendance
at Sunday Mass. He waited for a call that he hoped
would give him a role in the democracy that the revolution had promised.

But the only call was one from Dolores informing
him of a meeting of the Cuban Freedom Committee, to
be held on the last day of the month at María's house.
He arrived at her door with a heavy heart, not light-
ened by her warm greetings to the other members of
the committee, while barely making eye contact with
him.

Dolores began the meeting without ceremony.

"I want to tell you about a new project that I need
your help with. It's to—"

León whispered to Pedro, "Did you hear the terrible news about Camilo Cienfuegos?"

Dolores scowled at them like a strict schoolteacher
faced with ill-behaving students. "Do you gentlemen
mind? I'm talking!"

"I'm sorry," said León, "but I think we should all at least recognize that three days ago the revolution lost one of its greatest heroes in an air crash over the ocean."

"Yes, Camilo Cienfuegos was a big hero of Santa Clara, Dolores said. "But lately, he was acting a little too independently."

"What?" stammered León. "Why, I think he was probably Fidel's biggest booster."

"I'm told that he had plans to take over the revolution for his own ends," said Dolores, in a tone that brooked no argument.

Pedro stared at Dolores, so beautiful, so intelligent, so important to the revolution. But she seemed to have no conscience; to her death was inevitable, just another bump in the road.

"If I may get back to the subject matter of our meeting?" asked Dolores. "We must each organize a new committee in our home neighborhoods to document every block. Next year Fidel will announce the kickoff of this program nationwide. The program is going to be called Committees for the Defense of the Revolution or CDR."

"What will they do?" asked María.

"Help organize grassroots activities. By knowing who's living where and how many people are at each address, we can provide governmental services: health care, educational programs, etc."

"Like a census?" María persisted.

"No, not exactly. Each block will have a captain

who will inform the government of the needs of the people who live there, and also report any anti-revolutionary activities in their immediate neighborhood."

"So what are we to do?" asked Pedro.

"Map out the neighborhoods where you live. Identify likely block captains, and bring back their names and addresses. In a few months' time, we'll divide up and do training sessions for each of the block captains so they know how to form the local CDRs."

Pedro felt very uneasy. It seemed as if she were asking the committee to be spies for the revolutionary government.

When the committee took a break and León walked out to the terrace, Pedro followed.

"What do you think of these CDRs?" he asked, keeping his voice low.

"I think the idea stinks," León answered. The cigarette in his hand trembled. "If they want to provide government services to the people, there are easier ways to get the message out."

"That's what's been bothering me. I'm troubled that the captains are supposed to call government investigators. I'm hoping this committee idea will die a natural death. "

"I didn't sign up for this—it sounds like someone's been taking lessons from a Stalinist."

"Have you seen any changes at El Tribunal de Cuentas?" Pedro asked.

"It's difficult for me to say, but I've had some brief discussions with María about what our office should be doing in terms of inventorying the Batistiano assets that have been seized. She tells me that every time she suggests to Luis that accounts should be set up to track these assets, he puts her off."

At the mention of María's name, Pedro sighed. León could talk to her; he could not. He missed the intimacy that he had supposed would last forever.

"I just wish they'd give me a fucking job to do. I'm not accomplishing anything at Espíritu Santo."

"Whoa, Father! What would the sisters say? Setting up a government is a massive job. I suppose we just have to give it a little more time. But it is troubling, like some of Dolores's pronouncements. Fidel would not be in Havana today if it were not for Cienfuegos."

Pedro shook his head sadly. León had said just what he was thinking. As he walked into María's living room, he brushed by her Steinway and plunked a few keys.

The following day, Pedro conducted services as usual. The church was so crowded that a few had to stand behind the back pew. Cienfuegos's air crash had caused Fidel to declare a national day of mourning. Both men and women wiped tears from their eyes as they prayed for his soul. Pedro looked out at the throng and once more remembered how hard it had been for him to attract more than thirty parishioners less than a year before. Oddly, he didn't care. He went through the steps of the Mass by rote.

Dutifully, he waited outside the church door to

greet his congregation. This line will never end, he thought, as one after another approached him and shook hands. At last, he stepped out of the sunlight back into the darkness of the church. But not all of the crowd had left. María stood just inside the doorway, her head covered by a mantilla.

"Pedro," she said, grasping his hand, "we need to talk."

"Here? Now?" Pedro looked around. Miguel, Domingo, and a few altar boys were at the pulpit, returning the liturgical vessels to the tabernacle. "Meet me next door at my apartment. It's on the second floor, facing the street." Pedro's mind raced. Truly there is a God, he thought.

María was cradling his violin when he arrived upstairs, breathless. She threw her arms around him. Astonished, Pedro stepped back.

"I've made such a mess of my life!" she cried, pounding her fists against his chest. "We've been sold out by Fidel and Luis."

"What do you mean, my dear? What's happened?"

Pedro led her to his battered sofa, holding her hands in his. The relief that she had come back to him made him resolve that whatever it was that was troubling her, he would fix.

"Nothing has changed," she said. "Nothing. In many ways our life is worse. They're enlisting children in the militia, and I hear the firing squads are killing more people now than when Batista was here."

María got up and paced around Pedro's apartment.

Pedro worried. What would she think of the dirty dishes he'd left unattended for days in the sink, or his clothing strewn over several chairs?

"I thought they'd close La Cabaña, but it's busier than ever! Aren't you afraid?"

"No. What I am is bored. Dolores says to stay here, do my job, and be patient. If anything, the revolution is trying to forget me. But none of this is new. Sit down and tell me what's gotten you so upset today."

María rejoined Pedro and said in a slow, clear voice as if explaining something to a child, "There's something fishy about Cienfuegos's death. Also, the Fidelistas are beginning to nationalize private property. A coffee plantation owner I've known for years lost his land even though it was just a small place. And they've taken over the mines. Before long there will be no private enterprise. And if you complain—well, people simply disappear."

"Wait a minute, I know about the agrarian reform, but that's a long way from proving that there's no private property. No, you're not telling me what's really bothering you. No one gets this upset because a piece of land is being redistributed."

"We've been duped—we've all been duped, I tell you!" María's face reddened. She began to pace the floor again, in her agitation, bumping into a chair and knocking it over.

"At the office this week, I heard Luis discussing the need to take over a cattle ranch of a man I know, Fabian Guillama. It's not one of those huge ranchos—

only three thousand acres. But it's profitable. It's always been profitable."

"What does Luis want with it?" Pedro stifled a thought about hysterical women.

"He wants to turn it into a sugarcane field. The agricultural plan for this district is to have nothing but sugarcane."

"But why are you so panicky? The new reform law says that only farms bigger than thirty-three hundred acres can be expropriated."

María gave Pedro a look that seemed to say, "Dummy!"

"I made a mistake, a terrible mistake. I told Fabian about what I overheard. He made a scene at the National Institute of Agrarian Reform. Now Fabian's disappeared. His wife's in a panic. I'm in a panic. What if they find out that I was the one who told him about the plans to nationalize his ranch?"

"How would they find out?" Pedro could not help but think she was more concerned about herself than about her friend Fabian.

"Pedro, you don't understand—once you're charged, you're guilty. And once you're in La Cabaña, you'll say anything to get out."

Pedro understood those facts only too well.

"And this nonsense about a plane crash—we're a small island. Cienfuegos had an expert pilot flying from Santa Clara to Havana. Why would the plane even have flown over the ocean in the first place? And if it did, why has no wreckage been found? I'm telling you, Cienfuegos is in La Cabaña with my friend Fabian!"

Pedro interrupted María, fetched her a glass of water, and managed to draw her into his arms again. He felt her breasts push against him and the warmth of her breath near his ear. He kissed her eyes.

"Try not to be overly concerned about this. You'll make yourself sick. We don't know the whole story about Cienfuegos, but I'm sure León will find out."

Immediately she was contrite.

"I'm so sorry about all I said on *La Rosa Blanca*."

"I said a few things then that I didn't mean as well," Pedro replied, letting his fingers run through her hair. "Let's take this one step at a time."

No matter how out of whack our world is right now, holding this woman is what I was meant to do, he thought. She may have rejected me once, but I don't care. She says she needs me now, and I'm ready.

Chapter 24

The next morning Pedro called León at his office.

"Feel like some ice cream?" he asked.

"It's funny that you should ask that. I was with Fidel and Luis last night, and they were complaining that with Howard Johnson closed, it's hard to get a choice of flavors. Fidel plans on building a giant ice cream parlor that will dwarf anything that the gringoes ever had, because ice cream is a patriotic food made of cream and a lot of sugar," León remarked.

Pedro laughed at the thought of home-grown ice cream.

"Well, I'm not sure how many flavors are around, but the Tencen at Galiano and San Rafael will at least have chocolate and vanilla. I figure that's a ten-minute drive for both of us. Anyway, there's a matter of great urgency I need to talk to you about."

"Shall we say about two this afternoon?"

Pedro decided to walk. He had dressed in casual slacks and a short-sleeved guayabera shirt, hoping to blend in with the other pedestrians. It was a sunny afternoon with temperatures in the low eighties. Perfect sailing weather, Pedro thought. Yesterday, María had not been the same woman who had cavalierly dismissed him on their last voyage; maybe next time the sailing would have a happier ending. He felt intensely alive, thinking of the possibility.

Green-uniformed soldiers wearing prominent M-26-7 insignias around their upper arms were still stationed on nearly every street corner, all with bushy hair and beards, as if they were competing in some ill-conceived Fidel look-alike contest. Pedro threaded a path along sidewalks still littered with debris from the store lootings. Former upscale shopping areas were now shattered skeletons of prosperity. At several points along the street, barricades blocked traffic, and Pedro was glad he'd set off on foot. He arrived at the Tencen before León.

León drove up in a black Tribunal car, a 1958 Chrysler Imperial, with M-26-7 flags flying from masts on each of the front two fenders. León would have no trouble with roadblocks in that car, Pedro thought.

The Imperial's passenger window lowered and León called out, "Jump in, Padre."

"I thought we were having ice cream," said Pedro, climbing into the Imperial.

"It's probably better to be somewhere a little less public," León replied.

They drove silently through the crowded streets. Sure enough, the bushy-haired *barbudos* waved them through every checkpoint.

"You must stick out with your well-trimmed beard at the office," said Pedro, tweaking León's sculpted goatee. "The rest of the military has forgotten what a razor is used for."

"I give it until next summer. When the heat makes the streets here feel like an oven, suddenly it won't be so fashionable to look like a Neanderthal."

They arrived at a wharf where a ferry left for Regla. The ferry was tiny, a small rectangular barge, large enough for no more than sixteen. It was topped by a wooden shack, painted blue at some time in the distant past. Wind and sun had faded it to a hint of azure. The boat bobbed on the gentle waves of the bay. It was leaving in fifteen minutes for its short trip across the harbor, and León bought three tickets.

"Who's the extra ticket for?"

"Just wait a few minutes. A friend is entitled to a little surprise."

Although Pedro did not like surprises, he was willing to suspend his prejudices when moments later, a woman's familiar figure came running up to the ferry. María gave both of them a big hug, as if her appearance were ordained, and they walked onto the ferry and found a place in the small cabin.

Over the rumble of the ferry's engine, León told Pedro that María had related Fabian Guillama's plight to him, too. "So, I knew what your urgency was when you called."

Pedro felt a little jealousy strike him that María was broadcasting her plight to others than himself. "Do you agree with María that people's lives have not improved since the revolution?" asked Pedro.

"I've thought about that," replied León. "With any major change, one must expect chaos for a while until things settle down. Fidel promises a return to the constitution that Batista tore up. If that happens, then yes, I think things will be better."

María strained to be heard above the engines.

"Is this better? This morning at El Tribunal de Cuentas Luis was with Che in director Fernández's office. I could hear him screaming in his Argentinian singsong. Then, I saw a half-dozen assistant directors and Fernández being dragged off in handcuffs. How long until they come for me?"

"Don't you think you're exaggerating?" asked Pedro.

"Exaggerating?" María shot back. "No, absolutely not! Our new government wants to punish any behavior it deems counterrevolutionary. Che Guevara's credo has become, 'If in doubt, shoot.'"

"I'm hearing gossip, too, María." León looked sober. "I heard that Che uses the firing squads as psychological torture—lining up would-be victims and giving the order to shoot, followed by silence. The terrified victims either shit in their pants or faint, and have to be dragged back to their cells."

María immediately stood up, "I'm going to be sick!" The next moment, she was hanging over the railing.

The two men watched her with concern.

"Maybe in the long run, things will improve, but I believe that right now it's too dangerous for María to remain here," León said. Minutes later, when she returned, pale and stricken, they made some decisions.

León spoke to them both. "I have a friend at the American Embassy. When we get back to the dock, I want you to go directly to the embassy. They will arrange emergency visas for you and your family. Go home and collect the kids and then hide out until the night flight to Miami tomorrow."

María seemed torn between grief and belligerence. "Is this absolutely necessary? I must leave my homeland, this island where I've lived my entire life?" Her voice cracked. "I will never be able to return, you know."

"María, if Che finds out what you even think you know—you're a cooked goose," León said solemnly.

"But where am I going to go? I don't know anyone in the United States!" She stared out the window toward the mouth of the harbor and the sanctuary some ninety miles north...so close yet frighteningly distant.

Pedro thought fast. "Remember I told you that I went to the U.S. to study music when I was a kid? Well, I made a friend there who lives in Philadelphia now. It's been a while since we've talked, but I'm sure he'll help."

María was now trembling so that Pedro feared she would not be able to accomplish an escape. He took her hand.

"León's very wise. It's the only safe thing to do. Call me from the embassy and I'll give you my friend's name and address. I'll get in touch with him, and I know he'll sponsor you because he's a good guy."

María appeared to take herself in hand. "Okay, what must I do?"

"After you get the visas, bring your family to the church. You will be secure there until we can get you to the airport."

Their plans made, they were the last to exit the ramp after the ferry plied its way back to Havana. León and María drove away in León's official car. Pedro was quick to notice two men in ill-fitting business suits standing by the ticket booth, watching León's car depart. One was scribbling something in a notebook. He glanced at Pedro, but then jumped into a battered Ford parked in front of the ferry building, and sped off in the direction that León had taken.

Pedro dove into a crowd of pedestrians walking to Santa Clara Street and lost himself among them. The crowd thinned out, and Pedro headed across Inquisidor, glancing behind every few seconds. To be safe, he wove back and forth between streets, increasing his pace until he reached Ignacio Street, where he hurried home without incident.

Chapter 25

The phone was ringing. He glared at the intrusive demon on his desk. To silence it, he picked up the receiver.

"Father, it's been a long time!" Dolores Barré was trying to joke, a joke in itself.

"It's always nice to hear from you, Dolores," Pedro replied, ignoring her attempt at humor. "I'm actually glad you called. I'm still waiting to get a job so that I can get away from this church. Every day is torture."

"Patience, comrade. Trust me. You're a hero, and the revolution does not forget her heroes."

Pedro wished she would get to the point. She had become as much of a torture as the church, and the thought of having once succumbed to her sexual flair now embarrassed him.

"But we do have a little assignment that I need your help with now," she said, her voice dripping with honey.

He was immediately suspicious. Was this about María? His heart sank. To try a little humoring of his own, he asked, "How may I help you, comrade?"

"Remember when you came to La Cabaña to help with the execution of that Colonel what's-his-name?"

"Rojas." Pedro would never forget the man's bravery. At least she's in the dark about María, he rejoiced.

"Yes, Rojas—something like that. Well, we have another traitor who's going to be shot tonight, and Che wants a priest there for appearances sake."

"Unfortunately, since only the church seems to know I exist, I must work on a sermon for Sunday, and later I'm counselling a couple who is getting married. Tonight, I'm meeting a priest from the archdiocese, and I have an early morning appointment."

Dolores's tone quickly changed. "Comrade Father, I don't think you understand. When Che asks for something, it's an order. A car will pick you up at eleven P.M. You'll be home early enough to climb safely into your bed."

She hung up the phone. He immediately picked it up again and called his friend in Philadelphia. As always, Larry was a person he could depend on.

As promised, a Jeep with its telltale M-26-7 flag flying arrived at Espíritu Santo to whisk Pedro off for his third visit to La Cabaña. He had that familiar feeling of being a collaborator in a torture chamber and an enabler of death. It's true, he thought, I've known for a while that I was a fake priest, but now and much worse, I've found that I am an apathetic coward.

If the prison looked forbidding during the day, at night it was a medieval dungeon. In the courtyard, the cold spotlights illuminated the "wall" and the rats that scuttled in fear into the corners. Following behind a guard, Pedro confronted not only the hundreds of holes where bullets had scarred the wall during past executions, but fresh bloodstains that had been added to the dried matter. The stench was like that of a slaughterhouse. A few photographers and reporters hung about looking uncomfortable, there to record the demonstration of revolutionary justice.

The reporter from *Bohemia* was interviewing the ringmasters of the circus, Dolores and Che Guevara. Dolores, dressed in fatigues, looked unbelievably beautiful for such a horror show. She wore a black beret that matched Che's.

"Comrade," welcomed Dolores, "you've met *Comandante* Guevara?"

Pedro squeaked out, "Yes, good evening, comrade."

"Maybe not for everyone." Che grinned.

Pedro followed his escort to the same cage where Colonel Rojas had been held prisoner. Inside, the traitor lay on the ground—a boy, not more than fifteen, his bloody body writhing in pain in his own urine and feces. Pedro, swallowing the bile in his mouth, went to him and cradled his head. So children are now labeled traitors, Pedro thought. This half-dead creature would soon be joining Fernando, the poor, dead boy who had taught Pedro how to shoot.

"Help me, Father," the boy cried. "I don't want to die."

The boy reached up and grabbed Pedro's arm with such a final display of strength that Pedro was unable to withdraw his purple stole.

He began to cry weakly, a small dog's whimper. Pedro continued to hold his hand, his priestly duties forgotten forever.

"Shh, shh," he comforted. "We'll meet again in a far, far better place."

He held the boy until two soldiers came into the cage to drag him to his death. At the wall, they had to prop him against the wall like a rag doll that had come unstuffed. When the firing squad took aim, Pedro had to be restrained.

The officer in command cried out, "*Pelotón atención, preparen, apunten, fuego!*" Shots rang out, and the rag doll crumpled. Then, to Pedro's horror, the body began to twitch. The officer, a young lieutenant, who looked little older than his victim, approached the boy and drew his pistol to administer the coup de grâce. He took aim, his arm shaking wildly, but he fired and missed. The boy screamed in fear and agony. Pedro rushed to his side.

"Father, help me," the wounded boy whispered.

"The sentence has been carried out. Now free him and get him to a hospital," Pedro said quietly to the lieutenant. The officer looked over at Che Guevara, who was witnessing the scene. Che shook his head in the negative.

The officer said, "I'm sorry, Father, I can't do that."

The lieutenant's arm was still shaking as he pointed

215

the weapon again. Pedro had had enough. He grabbed the lieutenant's hand to steady it and pointed it at the boy's skull.

"Fire, you son of a bitch!" Pedro yelled. The pistol went off and, this time, the boy stopped moving. The explosion blew pieces of skull onto Pedro's robe.

He turned away to the mock applause of Che and the laughter of Dolores. God, if there is one, is going to punish me for letting these acts take place, much graver than any other sins I've committed, he thought. I'm as guilty as anyone else. He ignored the presence of the Jeep and walked away from the prison like a man unstrung.

At home, he removed his robe and burned it in the sink. He ripped the gold crucifix from his neck and threw it into the trash can. Then he opened a bottle of Chianti from Palermo, and drank until he fell onto the floor, his mind numbed, his pain temporarily eased.

He awoke early. Now, he must think of María—did she make it to the embassy? Did anyone see her go inside? Did she get the visas? So many things were going wrong, and he had no control over any of them. Light had not yet broken when he heard a car roll to a stop in the street below. It was María's Oldsmobile with the family inside. After he had ushered them into his apartment, he began to take charge.

"Give me the keys," he ordered María. "I want to ditch your car. Did you get the visas?"

"Yes, León's friend was very helpful," she said, her voice barely above a whisper.

"Then all we have to do is hide you until evening and then get you to the airport by seven P.M., an hour before the night flight to Miami. If we just take small careful steps, we'll get you safely out of here." Pedro tried to sound optimistic, but every part of his being shouted, "Failure."

"You make it sound so simple," she said. "And I wish you were coming." María reached out and touched his hand.

Pedro embraced her, saying, "Perhaps I can join you soon."

He did not kiss her, even though he was uncertain if he might do so again. Instead, he went out into the early dawn and left the Oldsmobile on a dead-end street next to an abandoned factory.

The day passed with eating and games of Monopoly.

"Say good-bye to your money," he teased the children as he rubbed the dice between his palms, before tossing them on the game board. Only María stared out the window, as if time were moving too slowly for her.

When León arrived, Pedro immediately knew that something was amiss.

"We're going to have to change plans," León announced, hiding his feelings behind a solemn face.

María instinctively gathered her children around her.

"They know," León said.

"Who knows what?" asked Pedro, his stomach twisting in a knot.

"Dolores—and probably Luis."

"Are you certain?" asked Pedro. Visions of the bloody wall at La Cabaña filled him with dread.

"I saw Dolores. She asked me why I had a sudden interest in Regla!"

María and Pedro looked at each other.

"She was just fishing," León continued. "She really doesn't know what she knows. Apparently, they've been watching the American Embassy. Everyone who enters is photographed. She saw your picture, María."

"What did you say?" asked Pedro.

"I made light of it. I told her that you weren't happy with your children's schooling and that you were looking into sending them off to the U.S. for the spring semester."

"What was her reaction?" asked María.

"She said that you're not going anywhere until Che asks you a few questions."

"Oh my God!" María began to sob, and the children came to comfort her. "It's all unraveling."

"One thing, for sure," said León. "They're going to be watching the airport. Don't even try to go there." He looked at Pedro. "There's only one solution to the problem, and you know it."

Pedro nodded his head.

"There's a certain poetic justice to this solution," Pedro said. "Now, after demanding for months that

218

Dolores give me something useful to do, without knowing it, she's done just that."

"What are you two talking about?" asked María.

"*La Rosa Blanca*," said Pedro, nodding with certainty. "Yes, she's the only way out."

León immediately made it plain he was going with them.

"But the government is not after you!" exclaimed Pedro. "We'll be all right."

"You, and a woman with three children in the middle of the Florida Straits—I'm not letting that happen. Besides, Dolores may be a lot of things, but she's not stupid. Before the day's out, she'll add up two plus two, and it will be me that Che will be interrogating."

"I don't have the energy to argue with you. When do we leave?"

"Immediately, if not sooner. There's no time to lose. I'll go buy whatever provisions I can find and—"

León was interrupted by a knock at the door, followed by Miguel bursting into the room. "Father, there are soldiers at the entrance to the church! They say they're here searching for a woman."

León caught Pedro's eye. "That didn't take long. Let me do all the talking."

At the main door of the church, two young soldiers flaunted the ubiquitous red-and-black emblem on their arms. They were bearded like virtually every other militiaman in the city. León confronted them.

"You two!" he shouted. "What do you want?"

"We…we…we've been…um…sent to…uh…

search the church," the rounder of the two stammered.

"Search the church for what?" the granite-jawed colonel asked, his chin jutting out in a challenge.

"We're, uh, looking for a woman. She's...she's wanted by El Tribunal de Cuentas."

"The revolution does not search churches. This is the Father. If you have any questions about a woman, ask him!"

The militiamen hesitated. Clearly, they hadn't been trained to address situations that controverted their orders. The heavyset man began, "Uh, Father, we were sent here to search the church for a woman, María Guerra. Is she here?"

"The only woman at the church is Sister Isabel. She looks after me and cooks. Right now she's whipping up some eggs for an omelet for me and my guest. If you comrades are hungry, perhaps you'd like to join us."

A look of concern came over León's face at Pedro's easy lies.

"No...uh, no...I don't think we can do that. Our orders—"

"Well, in that case, the colonel and I are going to eat. If I let her cooking get cold, Sister Isabel will skin me alive—there's nothing scarier than an angry nun," Pedro said.

"But...but...sir. We're supposed to look for ourselves," the fat soldier said.

"Do you know who I am?" the colonel broke in.

"Yes, certainly, *Comandante*."

"Now you two get out of here, and don't be bothering the priest and this church again."

His words had the desired effect. Without further comment, the militiamen got into their Jeep and sped off.

"Thank you, my friend," said Pedro, wiping his brow.

"What if they'd been really hungry?" asked León.

Pedro and the colonel traced their route behind the altar to Pedro's office.

"Thank you, Miguel," Pedro said to his assistant. "You can go now." Miguel left the office, gently closing the door behind him.

"God be with you," Pedro said sadly, as the door latched. They listened to Miguel's footfalls fading into the distance.

"You'd best be buying those supplies," Pedro said. "I've got a few things to finish up. When you're done, we'll meet at my apartment."

Stunned, Pedro reflected. Leaving Cuba—before that morning, the thought hadn't occurred to him despite his despair. Now he could think of nothing else. He drew paper from his desk drawer and hurriedly wrote letters to both his parents and his brother. He asked their forgiveness and pledged to someday return.

His last act was to call Domingo. Pedro would sorely miss the man he now considered a dear and close friend.

Domingo answered on the first ring. "Are you calling to invite me to lunch?" he asked, a hopeful chirp to his voice.

Pedro explained what he was about to do.

There was silence on the other end, but Pedro heard his friend's labored breathing. Finally, Domingo said sadly, "I'll miss you, my son." Then he gave him some final advice. "Remember to practice your English on the trip, and when you get to Florida, buy a dog. Everybody in America has a dog."

Chapter 26

The M-26-7 sedan raced the six of them through the empty streets of Old Havana. It was the first of December and not yet dawn, and the boats at their moorings were as still as the streets. Even María's children were awed into silence. Another of the ubiquitous military Jeeps was parked in the driveway of the club. Two soldiers slept in the Jeep, but woke with a start when they heard León's official sedan.

"The club is closed," said one of them, a sergeant.

Pedro took out the envelope containing his magic letter.

"I suggest you read this," said Pedro in the calmest voice he could muster.

The man's eyes glared at the paper until he got to the signature—Raúl Castro.

Instantly, the hostility disappeared. Again, the safe-conduct pass had worked its magic.

León stepped out next and faced the soldiers. Once more, his position in Castro's military proved as forceful as Pedro's pass. He saluted the guards smartly.

"Well, keep up the good work," he praised. "Meanwhile, my friends and I are going for an early-morning sail around the harbor. That is, unless you object."

"Yes, sir! I mean, no, sir!" the sergeant said.

Without a look backward, Pedro and León placed the supplies into a dinghy. Pedro rowed them out to where *La Rosa Blanca* quietly floated, moored to her buoy.

León chuckled. "We must remember to send Raúl a thank-you note."

Silently, María and her family made themselves comfortable in the forward cabin, while Pedro and León stowed their minimal gear. They cast off in a light breeze, and the sails began to fill. *La Rosa Blanca* slipped quietly out to sea.

The straits were a sleeping tableau, silently waiting for maritime commerce to come onstage at daybreak. In the distance, the lighthouse marking the entrance to the harbor winked its eye at the departing sailors. A foghorn sounded its lonely cry. *La Rosa Blanca* headed due north, the only ship under way.

Estimating that they were making about two to three knots in the light breeze, Pedro figured it would take them at least three hours to make it to international waters, so he left the running lights off. Switching them on would attract attention. Safer in the dark, he thought. We don't need to advertise our departure.

They had about ninety miles to sail to Key West by crossing the Gulf Stream. Pedro's history lessons at Belén had taught him that the Florida Straits were an equal-opportunity sinker of ships of all nations, including sixteenth-century Spanish treasure ships. But there was no way to get to Florida without crossing that body of water.

María joined Pedro and León in the cockpit. At that moment, Pedro had an epiphany. "I'll never sail from Havana harbor again," he said.

He looked back at the lights of the city that still twinkled in the predawn darkness.

"This oppression cannot last—you'll be back before you know it," said León. "Too many people died to make Cuba free. They'll never stand for another dictatorship."

"I'm not so sure," cautioned Pedro, uneasy with León's apparent optimism. León had never witnessed what he had in La Cabaña. "It's almost a year since Batista fled our shores, and the firing squads are still busy."

A splash off the port beam startled all of them. "What was that?" María asked.

"Probably a marlin gobbling his breakfast," Pedro assured her. "Fish don't worry about revolutions. They swim without a care, except for watching out for larger fish!"

"Speaking of eating," said León, "I'll be right back." He disappeared down the companionway and returned in less than a minute balancing cups, a Thermos, and a paper bag, followed by the children. While he poured the coffee, María took out a pastry the size of two hands. The children shouted at the sight of this enormous *Pan de Gloria*. Their eagerness made Pedro realize that he was hungry, too.

"Domingo would have done a somersault for one of these."

"That priest sure likes to eat," agreed León.

"With Domingo, dunking is a religious ritual—his own personal Eucharist." said Pedro.

"Who's Domingo?" asked María.

"He's a special friend who spends most of his time worrying about his next meal. León once brought him a beef tenderloin. I thought Domingo was going to break down in tears. You'll love him when you get to meet him." Pedro looked up to the heavens. "God willing that will be soon."

The sky began to lighten with a reddish glow. Mackerel clouds were scattered overhead. A jingle he had learned at Interlochen came to mind:

Red sky at night / Sailor's delight / Red sky at dawning / Sailor take warning."

Pedro stared at the sky.

"What's the U.S. like?" asked María. "It looks so big on the map."

"It's a beautiful country, except where it's too cold to think straight," said Pedro. "In Florida, you'll still think you're in Cuba—lots of beaches to sleep on and coconuts and oranges falling from the trees."

"I like the idea of a cold place—it forces one to work hard to stay warm. I want my kids to grow up where it's not so easy to be lazy."

"In Philadelphia, where Larry lives, they have some awful winters. If it's snow you want, that's where you'll find it."

"What do you think U.S. Customs will do with you and me ?" asked León. "María and her family have visas. You and I have nothing! Will they send us back?"

"The Americans are a sensible people. When they hear what we've been through, I can't imagine that they'll deport us back to Dolores and Che. Besides, God's been generous to my friend Larry. He can open many doors." Pedro crossed his fingers.

"I certainly hope you're right," said León. "I'm allergic to La Cabaña."

"Do you think the guards at the club have reported our sailing?" asked María.

"They will soon, and Dolores will get suspicious if we don't show up. But I think there are a number of places they'll look first," said León. "Remember, they don't really know whom to ask until they think of Domingo and Pedro's parents. It all takes time."

"I feel sorry for those two guards at the club," said Pedro. "When Dolores learns we didn't return from our day sail, she'll give them more than a tongue lashing."

Pedro thought back to the execution of the young boy at La Cabaña and Dolores's derisive laugh. "There's a ruthless side to her that is more than disturbing."

As the light of day illuminated the sea before them, Pedro focused on whitecaps that extended as far as he

227

could see. The wind blew stronger, and *La Rosa Blanca* knifed through the low chop.

I hope Dolores will take her time pursuing us, he thought. They've got some fast patrol boats, and we're not out of their range yet.

Chapter 27

La Rosa Blanca lunged forward, doubling her speed. At this rate, by sailing day and night with calm seas and a constant breeze, they could reach U.S. waters in less than two days, Pedro reckoned. However, he was aware that the Gulf Stream's strong current ran across their path. Unless he got it just right, they could be pushed way off course to the east, missing Key West and the mainland of the U.S. by hundreds of miles. Since the morning winds were from the west, Pedro took a northwesterly course, calculating that the Gulf Stream would push them east to make Key West without difficulty.

The children were sleeping below. María joined León and Pedro in the cockpit and, bracing herself on a stay, looked back at the faint line that was Cuba receding in the distance.

"I never thought it would come to this," she said, taking a handkerchief and blowing her nose. "To think of all that work in the Defarge Circle and afterward—I helped those bastards take over our country—we all did. And they pay us back by making us run for our lives?"

Pedro reached out his arm. "Come, my golden girl, sit by me."

Even sailing off into the unknown, Pedro had never been so happy. I would sail into Hell itself with her at my side. "How could you have known? All of us were misled."

Pedro and León scanned the horizon. Pedro figured they had traveled at least ten miles, and it was beyond his expectations that they hadn't seen a single boat.

"Enrique, what do you make of this? I was sure someone would come looking for us."

The colonel raised his binoculars. He scanned 360 degrees.

"Nothing!" he exclaimed. "Can it be this easy?"

The swells grew higher. *La Rosa Blanca* heeled sharply on the starboard side. At the bow, the waves seemed to dwarf the sloop, but as she rode through the troughs, she magically leaped over the crests, spray flying back into the cockpit. Above, clouds that at first light had looked like scattered stones now started to coalesce into tufts of darkening gray. Pedro estimated that the wind had reached fourteen knots. Noise from the hull was getting louder. The colonel trimmed the sheets, and Pedro scanned the horizon once more. Still no one there.

Around midday, María produced mugs of hot soup. The children scrambled up behind her. The girls started to scamper up to the bow deck, but León grabbed them back, as a wave doused all of them in cold spray.

"Father, can I steer?" asked Roberto.

"Don't bother the Father right now," admonished María.

"No, it's all right. He's old enough to help. But the girls will be safer below."

"That's not fair," Ruby pouted, her teeth chattering from cold.

"You two, follow the captain's orders," said María. "¡Vayanse!"

"Roberto, watch the compass needle and steer so we stay on a two-hundred-ninety-degree course," instructed Pedro.

María herded the two girls below, and in a few minutes, reappeared with sandwiches. Pedro looked at the sky. Had it been a normal daysail, he would have come about and made for home. The sky was threatening and it promised change. Change could be deadly.

As he watched the horizon, Pedro remembered preparing a sermon using a shipwreck as a metaphor for unnatural loss. It is an indifferent cataclysmic interruption, he had said. The drowning of a shipwreck victim goes unmarked. There's no body for the bereaved to bury and resolve their loss as happens when death strikes on land. As happened with us, Pedro thought, when Alberto died.

He turned his attention to Roberto's serious expression that, as he intently watched the compass needle and adjusted the helm of *La Rosa Blanca*, momentarily saddened Pedro. Helping one's family flee for its life should not be the occupation of a teenage boy. The children of Cuba deserved better.

"It's okay, Roberto, for the compass to go off a few degrees. All we need is to stay on a general course of two hundred ninety degrees. The heading will never be precise."

As the afternoon progressed, the sky continued to darken and the wind continued to build. The swells became deeper and broader. The bow would ride up the front of a wave and then crash into the following trough. As the sea built around them, a ghostly wind whistled off the stays. Roberto asked to be relieved, and Pedro sent him below to rest.

León occasionally used his binoculars to scan for other boats, but the fierce spray made the world indistinct. Clouds were now forming into dark gray cliffs. In the distance, a flash of lightning. Pedro counted the seconds until the clap of thunder. Eighteen, nineteen, twenty—almost four miles.

He decided to change course, taking *La Rosa Blanca* east northeast on a heading of forty-five degrees. Perhaps by turning away from the storm, they might be able to run around it. The wind shifted again to due north and, in spite of the spray, perspiration trickled down Pedro's back. The halyards began to clang against the mast and the wind, now at gusts of twenty knots, increased its spectral whistle. From time to time, the boat shuddered as it catapulted out of the sea on the front of a wave and came down on the trough behind.

"What do you think, Pedro?" León shouted above the din.

"Hold the wheel and stay on this course. I need to get a weather report."

"Aye, aye," León saluted.

Pedro grabbed the rail and went below. At the galley's table, he opened the hatch covering the radio. The tubes warmed slowly, as Pedro willed the instrument to come to life. Finally, the cabin filled with the sound of static and Pedro turned the tuner to isolate a frequency.

A voice in rapid Spanish—a Havana station—came into the clear. But it was just news about a big trial taking place. Pedro switched over to a ham band, and through the buzz of atmospheric distortion, he picked up a freighter somewhere near the Bahamas. It was reporting twenty-foot seas and winds of thirty knots. Pedro returned above decks.

"I think we need to furl the mainsail a bit," he cautioned. "Stay on the helm and I'll ease out the mainsheet. Head into the wind just enough to ease off pressure on the mainsail."

He knew his sailing skills were being taxed beyond his capacity. He also knew that only he could get them out of this storm.

Letting out the mainsheet, Pedro watched the sail start to luff like an infernal laundry line. Fearful of broaching, he let the boom swing out over the port beam as he inched his way forward to the mast. He managed to grab the halyard off the cleat and played it out, struggling to stay upright in the chaos.

The boom flailed about, then crashed down onto the transom, narrowly missing León's head, its aft end dipping into the sea. *La Rosa Blanca* heeled close to the crest of a wave. Pedro adjusted the halyard, grabbed an armful of sail, and brought the boom back amidships. But without the sail pushing them forward, the rudder was unresponsive.

Pedro pulled on the mainsheet with all of his strength, trying to capture the wind. The sail snapped taut, and *La Rosa Blanca* surged forward.

The sloop's speed increased. Pedro gasped in some needed oxygen, doused the jib, and collapsed next to León in the cockpit.

"Heavy winds," he reported soberly. Although it was only three in the afternoon, the dark clouds signaled evening. The seas raged around the boat, but she made steady progress in spite of the walloping from the waves. They had traveled at least fifty miles from Cuba, possibly a little more. Pedro took the helm.

León scanned the horizon again.

"Lights off the stern—one, maybe two boats." He pointed and shouted, "There!"

Rain had started to fall so heavily that it was difficult for Pedro to see clearly. But as they climbed the back of a huge swell, he spotted the lights amid the gloom. With no landmarks, it was impossible to tell in what direction the boats were headed.

In his anxiety, Pedro's hands slipped from the wheel, and the sloop veered into the wind. *La Rosa Blanca* slowed, as if dragging a deadweight. Realizing his error,

234

he quickly turned away from the wind. He looked back to where he'd last seen the lights—they appeared to have faded away. Whether they had been boats to save them or capture them, Pedro had no time to wonder now.

The swells had now reached twenty feet, Pedro guessed. When *La Rosa Blanca* descended down the back of one, the coming wave seemed as high as the spreaders. Water gushed over the bow and down into the companionway. They closed the hatches and León began to pump the bilge.

Pedro knew he needed help badly. He looked back over the stern, hoping there was a boat light behind him, friend or foe, but there was only rain and darkness. He despaired for an instant, then summoned León to the deck. He had to try the radio one last time.

Below decks, everyone was sick, vomiting, huddled together like animals. The once-clean galley was awash in floating gear. Pedro threw a length of line around his neck and switched on the radio. The minutes it took to come alive seemed like hours. One channel after another—nothing but squawks of electronic noise. In desperation, he switched to Channel 16, the international channel reserved for emergencies.

"Mayday, Mayday, Mayday!" he shouted into the microphone. Nothing but crackle responded.

"Mayday, Mayday, Mayday, this is *La Rosa Blanca* out of Havana!"

More crackle, then a voice.

"I'm coming for you, you son of a bitch priest!" Dolores's voice was unmistakable.

Pedro gasped—there was no escaping her. He dropped the microphone as if it were white-hot. I've got to do something, anything, he thought. I can't let that witch get her hands on María.

Regaining his composure, he picked up the microphone again and depressed the call button. "This is *La Rosa Blanca* out of Havana. We're a sloop taking on water, approximately fifty miles south of Key West. Women and children on board. Mayday, Mayday, Mayday!" He released the call button.

Crackles and pops from the radio's speaker. Finally, a man's voice: "This is U.S. Coast Guard cutter *Blackfriar* on station twenty-five miles southeast of Key West. Do you read me, *La Rosa Blanca*?"

A way out—from nowhere, here's a way out. Pedro turned toward the forward cabin.

"María! I need you to man the radio!"

The rain tore at their faces as León and Pedro fought to keep the sloop pointed into the swells. It was futile to further reef the mainsail. The wind whipsawed the sail and the boom. *La Rosa Blanca* valiantly tried to regain forward movement, but with each towering wave, she tossed around like a helpless baby.

Pedro had done everything he could think of. He had confirmed that María was at the radio keeping contact with the Coast Guard, that everyone's life jackets were secure. He had even managed to give the pale but still beautiful María a hungry hug and a passionate kiss.

Only one more chore remained.

"Go below and look after them," he ordered León. "And make sure everything is airtight. We're going to make this. Help is on the way."

León gave him a quizzical look, then an affectionate hug. He stumbled toward the companionway hatch and fought it open. Pedro found himself alone on deck, a lone victim of ferocious nature at its worst.

"Just like you, Dolores," he yelled into the wind.

He lashed himself to the cleats on either side of the wheel. The wind shifted again. *La Rosa Blanca* spun into a flying jibe. The boom swung from port to starboard in a split second. The whipsaw cracked the mast. Waves crashed over the gunwales and the boat wallowed. The force of the sea drove Pedro hard against the wheel.

Broken ribs, he thought, and gripped the wheel tighter, as if it were the only thing between him and perdition. He knew there was no hope for him now, but those below might survive. A fierce cracking that he took to mean the boat was breaking apart caused him to look upward. Through the wind and the water, he could make out the top of the mast, bearing all its hardware and lines, hurling toward him. The boom collapsed. Blood flowing into his eyes, he managed to release the cleated line that had lashed him to the wheel. The wind tossed him overboard like a discarded missal.

"God help me!"

A mountainous wave crashed over *La Rosa Blanca*,

slamming him against the hull. He barely struggled against the raging sea flooding into his eyes, his nose, his mouth.

Blessedly unaware of the welter of lines strangling him, pulling him ever downward to his doom, Pedro felt only relief.

"María, it is finished!" he cried out to the storm.

Then silently, like a penitent slipping into a confessional, he sank unseen beneath the welcoming waves.

Epilogue

THE GREAT DAY

Hurrah for revolution and more cannon-shot!
A beggar upon horseback lashes a beggar on foot.
Hurrah for revolution and cannon come again!
The beggars have changed places, but the lash goes on.

—William Butler Yeats

Acknowledgments

This is a work of fiction, and most of the characters who inhabit its world are imagined and are not intended to portray any real people who participated in the Cuban revolutionary movement of the 1950s. Of course, Fidel Castro, Raúl Castro, Che Guevara, and Cantillo are real; and the scenes in which they are found are based on historical fact.

I have learned in the writing of this novel that while writing is a lonely process, the final creation has many parents. A writer without an editor is like a sailboat without a keel and rudder. Fortunately, Barbara Phillips of Bridge Works Publishing is cut from the same bolt of editorial cloth as Maxwell Perkins, and her guidance to help me craft this story has been critically important. As my self-described "stern auntie," she has cut deeply when necessary and proposed alternatives that I would have been lost to find on my own. To the extent the writing is clear and entertaining, she is responsible. To the extent it's not, I bear full responsibility.

My literary agent, Jill Kramer of the Waterside Literary Agency, has been faithful and persistent in her drive to find the light of day for *Island of the White Rose*. Without her able assistance, this story would have been stillborn. I am grateful for all of her help, given unselfishly at all hours of the day and night.

I am also fortunate to have Asunción Ferrer in my life, a beautiful muse who inspired me to write the story of her mother, Alicia Marín, who dangerously led a double life in Batista's El Tribunal de Cuentas and the Fidelista underground in Havana. The character María is loosely based on parts of her life. Asunción has been a bottomless source of historic detail to hang on the skeleton of *Island*'s plot. For both her love and support during the writing and editing of *Island*, I am truly blessed.

Finally, my assistant, Sonya Aflleje, has been a patient listener and resilient sounding board when I have written myself into a corner. Her free spirit and creativity to help me think through my characters' personality flaws and peccadillos were invaluable, while helping me run a law firm to pay the bills during the writing of *Island*.